JUICY EROTICA

27 Succulent Stories

edited by Alison Tyler

Published by Accent Press Ltd – 2008
ISBN 9781906125875

Printed and bound in the UK by
Creative Design and Print

Cover Design by
Red Dot Design

Twelve new titles for 2008

Bad Girl

Seriously Sexy One

Naughty Spanking One

Tease Me

Down and Dirty One

Seriously Sexy Two

Juicy Erotica

Satisfy Me

Naughty Spanking Two

Seriously Sexy Three

Down and Dirty Two

Seduce Me

For more information please visit
www.xcitebooks.com

Juicy Erotica

We stop at farmers' markets whenever we're on the road, especially in August when the peaches come ripe, timed with the annual meteor showers. We get enough fruit to sate any summer hunger, not just peaches but whatever is juicy and sweet, bearing it away in brown bags like we are smuggling jewels. At the bed and breakfast we get a room overlooking the Pacific – we can see it from our bed and from the huge Jacuzzi in the bathroom. It's the honeymoon suite, though we are not married, just fucking like it's the only thing we will have to do for the rest of our lives ...

For SAM

Contents

Introduction

Confession time. Some of my dirtiest, *very* dirtiest, deeds ever have involved food. I've licked honey off a lover's flat belly, have drawn pictures with icing on a voluptuous vixen's naked inner thigh, and have had the pleasure of being turned into the most dreamy sort of after-dinner confections, myself. In my erotic cooking endeavours, I've employed Popsicles, chocolate, whipped cream, nectarines, oh, yes, and a vibrantly scarlet Cherry Slushee.

And the thing is – it's not just me …

Food and sex are fiercely entwined in many people's fantasy repertoires. Who hasn't bitten into some deliciously indecent dessert and felt those familiar flutters of pure ecstasy? And aren't those flutters similar to sexual sensations? Of course, I'm talking about only the best desserts … and the best sex, which is exactly where the concept for this anthology began. I wanted to gather a collection of the juiciest tales, food-related, and sex-infused to share with those whose fantasies meld with my own.

But as I read the submissions for this book, I realized that each writer has his or her own sweet tooth when it comes to luscious fantasies. Although my original call was for "erotic fruit stories," my authors over-rode the boundaries with their submissions. At first, there were the insistent demands: by scientific definition, an olive is a fruit, right? So is a tomato. And would fruit-flavoured cough-drops count? How about shoes that had fruit on them?

Ever more creative stories flooded my mailbox. Some authors chose to described sex using food descriptions, as

1

in Sage Vivant's joyful "Juice for Breakfast." Others compared food with sex, as in M. Christian's wildly satisfying "The Naked Supper." Certain authors focused their interested on what happens *after* a meal, such as the character in Rachel Kramer Bussel's "Doing Dishes." And some stories positively push the envelope. After reading Maxim Jakubowski's "Dear Alison," you'll see what I mean.

One thing is for certain, a smorgasbord of tantalizing tales awaits you, a topsy-turvy buffet of stories organized in a nouveau-style menu of selections. This is a gourmand's assortment, a taster menu, filled with a range of desires to satisfy the most discerning palate. Food is the catalyst to take the reader to the top, and over, savouring each word as if it were a fantastic morsel.

Whatever the particular food fixation – or sex fixation – the mouth-watering stories in this anthology share one common bond: Each is undeniably tasty with detailed descriptions that are destined to whet your appetite for far more than your next decadent meal …

Bon Appetit!
Alison Tyler

Farm Fresh
by Dante Davidson

"Juicy."

"Plump."

"Luscious."

"Mouth-watering."

"Delicious –"

I was rock-hard by the time I got to the farm. The words appeared on old-fashioned "Burma-shave style" signs, hand-painted in a startlingly bright red on small squares of yellow cardboard. The signs stood in a lopsided line by the side of the road, and their faux innocent words had gotten to me. Again. Gotten to me as they did nearly every day on my commute home from work. I knew it didn't make much sense. Why was I aroused by a series of adjectives used to describe fruit? It's not as if I'm the type of geek who uses a thesaurus to turn myself on, and clearly whoever had created these signs had possessed a good friend in Roget's.

But there it was – sense or no sense, I possessed a raging erection that made it difficult to continue driving, coupled with an undeniable desire to pull over and try the new crop of strawberries. Maybe that's all I needed. More fruit in my diet. Never seem to make that five-a-day goal. Perhaps an apple a day, or a strawberry or two, would deflect my ever-growing libido.

And maybe the girl would be there. Maybe the girl had something to do with it. She was a stunning blonde with a goddess body and long wave of blonde hair, and she stood at the ready behind the counter at the fruit stand. At least, usually, she stood there. Occasionally, I'd catch her walking out to the fields, and I'd note the way her hips moved under her faded jeans. Sometimes, she even seemed to notice me back, watching until I turned the corner and lost sight of her in my rear view mirror.

Why hadn't I stopped before now? I don't know. Desire to be home and end my day for real would win out over potential embarrassment as I shared my erection with a brand-new friend. Now, in the late spring sunlight, I felt as if the time had finally come.

It took me a few minutes to get myself under control before I exited the car and walked to the produce stand. And then instantly I realized all that deep breathing and thinking about baseball had been a waste. Here I was, hard all over again. Not because of any signs. Or because I have a hard-on for fresh produce. But because of her. Fact is, I could have used every one of those words to describe her. Ripe.

Juicy.

Ready.

Sweet.

She smiled when I approached, and then she raised a hand to me, as if we were old friends. I gave her what must have been my most baffled expression. Was she beckoning me to do her? That's what I was hoping, because it was clear in my mind how we'd make it work. Shove the berry baskets aside, pluck her up onto the counter, and ravish that sweet, ripe body of hers.

"Taste?" she asked, and my vision went blurry. Taste? Yeah, I wanted a taste. I wanted to start at her lips, which were bare of any cosmetic, but full and plump and pink. And then I wanted to move along the hollow of her throat, to drink in deep of her peaches-and-cream complexion. She was wearing a little white apron over a blue-and-white checked shirt. She had on faded jeans and tiny hoop earrings, and every time she moved, she made me want her even more. The way she pushed her wheat-gold hair out of her eyes. The way she seemed to possess a berry-hued blush in the apples of her cheeks. She was a meal. A meal at a five-star restaurant. And she was out here on the farm.

I wanted to devour her.

"Taste," she repeated, no longer asking a question. I saw now that she was offering samples, and I stepped forward and put out my hand. "You're from the city," she said, and when my eyebrows went up in a query, I saw her motioning to my sports car out in the dirt lot.

"Yeah," I said, embarrassed.

"You don't get quality like this from the supermarket," she assured me. "For the best taste, you need to come out to the farm."

"Let me judge," I said, teasing her. Of course, I was prepared to assure her that anything she put in my mouth was heavenly, but I wanted to hear her keep talking. She had a slice of peach ready and waiting, and she handed it over quickly. I took a bite, felt the juices swell in my mouth, and thought about what it would feel like to peel down her jeans and lick the split of her body.

"Sweet?" she asked.

I nodded.

"Then try this —"

Next was a berry, the ripest, roundest, most perfect

5

strawberry I'd ever seen. I greedily reached for it, but now the girl was teasing me. She held the berry just out of reach, and said, "What will you give me if I'm right."

"Right?"

"About this being better than any berries you've had in the city."

"What do you want?" I asked.

"Ride in your car."

I smiled. She was no hick. Yes, this was a farm, but it was a farm on the road between two major Northern California cities. The girl had seen plenty of fancy cars before, and probably driven in several. Maybe her family even owned one. With her good-looks, all the guys at the film studios right over the hill must have been hounding her for years. But I played along. She wanted to be country mouse, I'd be her city mouse without batting an eye.

"You got it," I told her.

"Have to play fair," she said. "You have to tell me for real if this is the sweetest fruit you've ever had."

And then she pushed it forward, and I put the whole strawberry in my mouth and bit down. Trust me when I saw that this was by far the most delicious piece of fruit that I've ever tasted. Trust me again when I say that she could tell by my expression I was hungry for far more than her Fruit Stand could provide,

"You win," I said softly.

"I think we both will," she told me, untying her apron and coming out from behind the counter.

"Can you just leave?"

"I can do whatever I want," she said, and I could hear the sound of a rebel in her voice. I liked that tone a lot. "Just give me a minute." I nodded, and then watched her hurry to the house behind the stand, and I prepared myself for being chased by some old hillbilly with a shotgun. But no, a pretty girl – sister? Mother? – came out with her and took over her spot at the stand, and then my blonde goddess rushed her way over to me.

"Where to?" I asked, ushering her to the car.

"I've seen the way you drive," she said, and I realized she'd caught sight of me slowing down to gaze at her. That I wasn't so top-secret after all. "Why don't you let me take you for a spin?"

Without a thought, I handed her the keys, and within moments, she'd motored us along a back road to an empty spot overlooking a flower-filled meadow. It would have been a lovely place to picnic, or to set up an easel to paint, or to –

"Taste?" she said, in the exact same way she'd offered me that first bite of peach, and now I looked to see that she'd split her jeans and was staring at me with a hungry, yearning expression that had to have matched my own. Matched, and perhaps surpassed.

I didn't answer this question with words. I answered it with my tongue, pressed to the split of her panties, where I could already make out the scent of the first juices of her arousal. For the first time, I realized how much like juices a woman's liquid was. I breathed in deep and thought of fragrant ripe fruits, thought of the berries and peach that I'd consumed earlier.

Crazy, but there was something again so fresh about her. So untouched and unmanufactured. My mind took me on a memory trip of the perfumed city girls I tend to go for. The tall lean ones with minty-clean breath and carefully blown-out hair. The ones who won't go out in the rain in case they get 'the frizzies.' And then I looked up at this girl, and I said, "Let's get out," knowing somehow that she would roll in the dirt with me if I

7

asked. That she would get all sloppy and messy and wet and everything would be fine.

More than fine.

She moved faster than I did, coming around to my side of the car and grabbing my hand. She brought me after her to the centre of the field, where a tree stood, gnarled by winds and time. Beneath it, she turned around, so that I could see her before she began to undress. Now, she moved slowly. Letting me see. Letting me appreciate the show. Her checked shirt popping open button by button. Her jeans sliding down her long, lean thighs. Then her white bra and panties, a simple matched set, carelessly strewn on the ground. I was behind her, still dressed in my suit and unprepared for what it would feel like when she came naked into my arms.

Sure, my fantasies had gotten me to this point. But reality can blow you away. Think about it: picturing a ripe strawberry will make your mouth water. Biting into one is an entirely different experience. And I was ready to bite into her. To bring my mouth to the rise of her shoulders and nip at her. To move in a line down her flat belly until I was kneeling on the dirt, pressing my open, hungry mouth now to the naked skin of her sex.

So this is what I did. Everything that her signs had made me want to do. She was juicy. And sweet. And ripe. She was succulent and mouth-watering, and –

"Delicious," I murmured, and she gripped onto me as I ate her. I pressed my tongue up inside of her pussy, drove it deep in there to get the sweetest tasting juices I'd ever savoured. She moaned softly as I brought her ever-closer to climax, and her noises simply urged me on. The intensity of the moment filled my head. How pure it seemed to be fucking outdoors. How smooth her skin was under my fingertips. Part of me couldn't believe this was real, and part of me knew not to analyze any more, but to give in, and to drink in, and to dine.

The taste of her was pure sweetness. The sensation of her cunt against my tongue was as unbelievable as was her next statement. "I want to come on you —"

Oh, god, I thought. I want that, too.

"I want to milk your cock," she murmured.

I ripped out of my clothes, tossing down my jacket for some sort of cushion against the dirt, and then waiting only long enough to see in her eyes what she wanted. I sucked in my breath as I lay down on the dirt and let her get between my legs. She was a vixen, her lips parting around my cock and drawing me in, giving me a slow, long lick and a short, firm suck. She worked me up and down, using her fingertips to stroke my balls, cradling them in the palm of her hand as she continued to play those naughty games with her mouth. When she'd gotten me was ripe as she wanted, she climbed astride, her body opening up and taking me deep within her. I knew she wanted to control the ride. I don't know how. I just knew. Maybe from the way she'd handled my sports car. Or maybe from the sparkling light in her eyes. I didn't care who was in the driver's seat this time. All that mattered was the way her pussy squeezed and released, the way her hips bucked up and down, the weight of her like a warmth on me I'd never felt before.

She leaned forward, her hands on my shoulders, and she rocked her pelvis against me, back and forth, and I could tell from the look on her face each time her clit got contact with my body. It was like an electric flicker passed through her eyes, making them a brighter blue, momentarily rivalling the sky before they settled back to their normal, deep colour.

I thought of what she said — the word she'd used —

"milking" – and that's what it felt like. Her pussy squeezed me so perfectly, over and over, until I knew just one more moment and I would come. I put my hands around her waist, moving her slightly faster, and she understood, and I saw her concentrating as I said, "I'm going to –"

She said, "Yes –" her breath a rush.

"Now," I said.

"Yes!"

And we reached it, with me bucking off her the ground, raising her up in the air as I came, and her finding her space a moment after, so that her cunt held me tight as I crested back down. Back down to a level that was still higher than any previous plateau.

The sky was that periwinkle blue of twilight as she came into my arms, her hair spreading over my naked chest, her pert body still sealed to my own. She looked directly into my eyes, and again I saw a glint of a rebel – or maybe a full-fledged rebel – gazing at me. And I saw those words again in my head. Ripe. Succulent. Juicy. All of them. All of them were her.

"See what I mean?" she said afterwards, her lovely blonde hair falling forward over her face. I reached out to brush away those corn-husk soft tendrils, and I raised my eyebrows, waiting for her to continue. "The fresher the better. Can't get quality like that in a sterile city environment, can you?"

Now, I understood, and I shook my head. "You're right," I agreed, smiling. "The only way to go is farm fresh."

Sweets For The Sweet
by Isabelle Nathe

People tease me constantly about my incredible sweet tooth. I must have one, right? I work in a candy store, after all, a tiny shop located on the outskirts of Santa Monica called 'Sweets for the Sweet.' Daily, I am surrounded by the most insane, fantasy-inducing confections: melted chocolate drizzled over hazelnuts, marzipan treats shaped by hand into decadent designs, hard butterscotch squares spilling over with thick liquid cream centres. But I've got will power. I never give in to my longings.

At least, not before the new girl arrived.

Jacques Merlhou is the French-born owner of the candy store. He decided in his usual flamboyant way that we needed extra help during our busiest time of the year – the ever-romantic Valentine's Day rush. "Oh, Naomi," he moaned, "we'll never make it on our own. We need another hand, don't we?"

I shrugged. I don't mind working hard, but I don't mind help either. I have no ego involved in my job, feel no threat from a fresh new employee. It's not as if I'm staking my place in a cut-throat competitive career. I work in a candy store, not on Wall Street. But maybe I should have paid more attention to Jacques, to his extravagant gestures as he spoke and to the way he eyed me carefully for my response. My boss likes to think of himself as Cupid. He knew full well that I'd been between girlfriends for awhile now. Perhaps he hoped to bring in more than an extra employee over the scarlet-hearted holiday season.

He is French, non?

Almost immediately, Jacques announced that the search was over. Again, my sensors should have been vibrating more raucously than a pager in my pocket, but I wasn't in the frame of mind to pick up on any amorous indicators. I only half-paid attention as Jacques, beaming with pride, informed me that he'd found the perfect new member for our team.

"You'll love her," he said, running his fingers through my thick dark hair, as if he wanted to make sure I'd give a good impression. I smiled easily at him, remaining my usual calm, collected self. To my surprise, he even pinched my cheeks gently, to force a flush. He can be so silly that way, always fixing every last detail, from the pure white icing on a tiny chocolate heart, to the lace-edged hem of my apron. On this day, however, he needn't have bothered. When I saw Julia, I flushed just fine on my own.

"She's here," Jacques told me breathlessly, pointing as Julia walked through the door, accompanied by the tinkling sound of the jingle bells tied to the handle. When I saw her, I found myself both confused and conflicted. Yes, I can face away from a plate of freshly created chocolate bonbons without a problem, but could I turn away from her? She was far more delectable than any candy I'd ever seen.

Tall and sleek, she sported a fiery mass of red curls

worn up high on her head, revealing a stunningly long neck, dainty collarbones, and the finest sprinkling of freckles on her pale skin. Her ripe round breasts were clearly outlined beneath her formfitting cherry-red blouse, and her high-class ass filled out the rear of her short tight crimson skirt. To complete the outfit, she had on white fishnets and stacked heels that accentuated her racehorse legs.

Without seemingly aware of my instantaneous attraction, she put out a hand and took mine in hers. I continued to stare, realizing that she embodied a term we use often at the candy store, but one that I never had put on a human before – simply put, she looked good enough to eat.

"Naomi, this is Julia," Jacques gushed. "She was trained in France, and she's here to help during the holiday rush."

"The holiday rush," I repeated dumbly, while my mind faltered, suddenly unable to make any polite chitchat. Precisely *how* would she help is what I really wanted to know. Help me to come in every single fantasy that flitted through my filthy mind from the second I saw her? Help me to lose myself in the dirtiest daydreams of all time when I was supposed to be working?

As she murmured something about how nice it was to meet me, I saw her pinned down on my bed while I took advantage of her breasts and her plump, full mouth. We would look good together. With my dark hair and burnished brown skin, and her red spill of curls and ivory-pale body – we'd complement each other easily. But there was much more to my instant fantasy than how pretty we might appear on a sheet-strewn mattress – I saw my chest of toys open, a long pink jelly dildo working in one fist while I parted her pussy lips with the other. I saw the two of us in a sensuous sixty-nine, her wet mouth open on my sex while my tongue thrust inside of her, lapped at her until she bucked her hips and came. Where Julia was concerned, there were no limits on my mental creations. Her pert nipples demanded clothespins, or simple silver clamps fitted with a fine chain. Her pussy needed attention, as did that ripe, round ass of hers. Would I spank her before or after? Would I make her beg me to take her ass, or would I simply part her cheeks wide and dive inside? I knew what that would feel like, could sense somehow the exact way to prep her, using my tongue and my thumb before introducing her to the wonders of my strap-on cock and an ocean of glistening lubricant –

I'd never had such an instant reaction to a girl before. All I could hope was that my gaze didn't give me away, that when she saw me staring at her, she wouldn't immediately know I was not only undressing her with my eyes, but that I was fucking her with a hearty seven-inch moulded cock, that in my fantasy world I'd not only made her come twice already with my fingers, fist, and tongue, but that I was now mentally drizzling warm melted chocolate sauce in the hollow of her belly and licking every inch of her clean.

She would be a dessert I wouldn't be able to say no to.

"Go to it, my sweet mademoiselles," Jacques cooed. "I'm sure the two of you will be best of friends in no time." And then, before disappearing into the back room, he called back to me, "Naomi, you show her the ropes, won't you, doll?"

Oh, Jesus. *The ropes.* That was a delightful new thought. The lithe young Julia tied down, her slim wrists above her head, her thighs spread wide while I played the most indiscreet sorts of games with my tongue in her pussy. I thought I could smell her from where I stood, the secret scent of her, even above the sultry notes of chocolate that always permeate the candy store. It took every ounce of my strength to finally let go of her hand, which I'd been squeezing far too tightly, and to welcome her to the store. I'm sure that she thought I was cold, and perhaps even dark-tempered. At the very least, she might have thought that I was jealous of her arrival on my territory. Because on that first day, every time she sent a smile in my direction, I felt my face harden. Why – when all I wanted to do was melt before her, or make her melt for me? Simple, I couldn't reveal my hand so quickly. What if she turned me down? What if she didn't swing my way?

Our first shift together was a pleasure-filled hell, as I tried to act professional and explain the job, while all I could think of was excusing myself to go and get off in back of the store, my own thighs spread, fingers working fast on the melting candy centre of my core. Luckily, Julia didn't need much guidance. She took over her position easily, and she was as sweet-natured as I imagined her pussy to be.

"Am I doing okay?" she asked me on her second day.

I nodded and tossed my dark hair back out of my eyes. Julia took a step closer and used her own fingers to work my long wisp of hair back behind my ear. "You're sure?" she said softer. "I'm not pushing you, not getting in your way?"

"No," I assured her. "No, not at all." I heard the ice in my voice, and wished I could do or say something to make her see what it was I wanted and why I was acting so tongue-tied. She widened her eyes for a moment, then shrugged and gave me an odd sort of look, and when Jacques walked in I saw him glance from her to me and back to her again.

By the third day on the job, she danced around me and Jacques as if she had always been there. We were a perfect team, in all but one way. Every time I looked at her, I saw her in another mental sex movie. Opening herself up for me. Beckoning me to come inside. When she moved next to me behind the glass counter, I could think only of spreading her out on the cool, glass top, of lifting her sea-green skirt and checking out what colour panties she had on beneath. I knew they would be filmy silk, trimmed with lace, and I envisioned pushing those panties to the side and searching out the mouth-watering treat between her thighs. I wanted to dine on her, to ravish her, to eat her from the inside out.

Jacques called her into his office just before quitting time in the middle of the week. They had a hushed conversation behind closed doors, and when she came out, she gave me a look of understanding that made my cunt throb. What had he said to her? I could only imagine. Jacques is well-skilled in the art of seduction. It must have been killing him to see me floundering. Had he truly played Cupid for me? And if so, what was her response to the arrow shot from my heart to hers?

She said nothing to me that night, but the next morning – on Valentine's Day – her attitude to me seemed to have changed. I began to think that perhaps she might feel the same way herself. We worked so easily together in a tantalizing tango. Occasionally brushing up against one another. Holding each other's gaze for a beat longer than necessary. There was a powerful connection between us from the word "go." One that was so strong I could practically taste it.

"Sweets for the sweet?" she asked me at the end of the night offering over a sample of one of the chocolate dream puffs she'd just created.

I shook my head.

"You're over chocolate?"

"After working here for three years, I truly couldn't eat another bonbon if you paid me."

"You're serious?" she asked.

I nodded.

"But they're divine. I can't seem to stop snacking." She licked her lips as if to prove the point.

"I know," I said, "But I gorged myself in the first month on the job. Now, I'm immune. I did the exact same thing back in high school, working the popcorn counter at the local revival house. When others drool over the smell of salt and melted butter, I can shrug, untempted."

Julia's grey eyes flashed. "But there are *other* confections –" she said, waving one delicate hand over the variety of items displayed for sale. My eyes didn't follow her gesturing fingers. I stared only at her as I nodded.

"Don't you see?" she said softly. "Don't any of them appeal to you?"

"Yes," I smiled. "Some do. One in particular definitely does –"

The instant blush to her lovely porcelain skin let me know that she had read my X-rated thoughts. Or at least, she was privy to the most obvious ones. The baser ideas that I had couldn't be so easily discerned, I was sure. Those would come later. After. But would she respond as I hoped? Was she as interested in me as I was in her? My heart pounded in anticipation, and I gazed at her freckle-covered cheeks, imagining that she had been dusted with the fine shavings of chocolate truffles. *Oh*, did I want to taste her. I don't think I've ever wanted anyone else quite

17

as much. My hunger pulsed within me. I knew my cheeks were flushed, could feel the heat radiating from my skin.

"What about this?" she asked, bringing forth a sliver of candied orange, its rind coated in a casing of rich white chocolate. I shook my head, then moved to the front of the store and ever-so-casually flipped the 'closed' sign out. Jacques was away playing Cupid with his own beau. It was the end of the day. Nothing else could stop me.

"This?" she asked next, holding out a cream-filled treat that I'd made myself.

"Something like that," I agreed. "Creamy inside. So creamy. And sweet."

"Oh, god," she sighed, and the candy fell from her hand as I made my way towards her.

"Sweet," I repeated as I lifted her around her slim waist and hoisted her up on the counter. She spread her thighs willingly, and I pushed up her skirt and received my first peek at the wonders beneath. I'd been wrong in my assessment. She wasn't wearing silk panties. Nor satin ones. Or even the plain cotton variety that are charming to discover every once in awhile. No, Julia had on something even more fucking sexy – and that something was nothing.

With her skirt up to her waist, I had a clear view of her naked pussy, shaved entirely and adorned with the sweetest drizzling of rhinestones. I'd heard of this sort of treat before – called "bare with a flair" – but I'd never come across a girl who'd gone in for the trend. In my opinion, it takes a very special sort of lady who will adorn her pubic region. One who must give a lot of thought to how she looks between her legs, and how others will think she looks, as well.

I thought she looked amazing. Just as our customers

18

tend to ooh and aah over our most intricately designed chocolates and marzipan, I oohed and aahed over the delightful image of her crystal-covered cunt. The smoothly shaved skin of her sex was decorated in a heart-shape, so well-suited for the Valentine season, and I bent down and flicked my tongue so lightly over those raised jewels, making her arch her back and push forward. She obviously wanted to feel my tongue warming an entirely different treasure – the gem of her clit, which I sensed was now alive with anticipation between her sleek pussy lips.

Although I had refused the different sugary candies she'd offered me earlier, I had no plans on refusing this. With a quick breath in of her glorious scent, I brought my lips to her pussy and licked. And oh, fuck, that first elegant taste just about floored me. I've watched our customers roll their eyes at the samples we offer. Licking their lips and sighing at the true luxury of the first bite of a double-cream, liquor-filled bonbon. My expression must have echoed that sort of pleasure. That deepest of pleasure that can only come from tasting the richest, most tantalizing dessert.

Now that I'd had my first introduction, I wanted more. Bringing my hands into play, I spread open her lovely lips and used the flat of my tongue to caress her clit. I lapped up and down, then pressed forward, covering her entire clit with my tongue and holding steady. I wanted her to feel the warmth and the wetness, and I also wanted to bring forth the richest of creams from her dreamy liquid centre. Julia groaned out loud and ran her fingers through my hair. She lifted her hips up to meet me, and I slipped my hands under her gorgeous ass and cradled her while I continued to dine. I had been waiting for this moment for less than one week, but it felt as if this encounter was years in the making. I wouldn't be rushed, not by her insistent fingers twining through my dark hair, not by her breath as it sped up to show her excitement. Not by anything. I needed to savour every single moment, every lap of my tongue on her clit and inside her. Every thrust of my face against her pussy, bringing forth the sweet juices that I had fantasized about from the moment I'd seen her walk through the door.

"Jacques said –" she murmured as she started to come.

"Said?" I repeated, my breath against her inner thighs, my fingers trembling as I found her clit and pinched it firmly.

"The two of us together would be, oh, god, oh, Naomi–"

I lapped harder at her as I felt the power of her climax flood through her pussy. "Sweets for the sweet," I finished for her, before ringing her clit with my mouth and swallowing every last drop.

Appetizers
by Simon Torrio

Standing before the wreckage, I feel an overwhelming wave of sadness that such a tragedy has come to pass. Sullied china scatters across a red-stained white cloth. Twisted metal implements are smeared with a curious mixture of colours. Candles stand like broken torches, guttered out at the height of their power by the sweep of human flesh in the throes of sudden helplessness. Fragrant flowers, ruined in their moment of triumph, lay sprawled across despoiled white, their translucent viscera running down, still, in diamond drops onto the floor.

Yet the tragedy persists: We didn't even make it to dessert.

Iris showed up at eight, eyes full with the emptiness of her belly. She'd worn a very tight dress as I requested: Skin-tight and pale peach, plunging deep in the front and revealing the ripe orbs of her breasts. I wore a clean white apron, black slacks, a white shirt and black tie. I had a white cloth draped over one arm.

"Your table is ready, Ma'am," I said to her. "May I take your coat?"

She smiled, amused at the costume I'd donned for the

evening. She handed me her coat and I hung it in the closet near the front door. She followed me into the depths of my apartment, finding the table set with one place, the head of the table. I pulled out her chair and she sat down.

Before she'd had a chance to adjust herself, I seized her wrists and produced a pair of handcuffs from my apron pocket. She barely knew what was happening before I had her wrists cuffed to the back of the chair.

"Hey!" she said. "What's going on?"

"Dinner for one," I said. "Look, ma, no hands."

Her eyes narrowed and her face reddened slightly. I saw the peaks of her breasts harden slightly under the peach-coloured dress. She relaxed, immobilized, into her chair.

"All right," she said. "I'll play. I'm hungry enough."

"Yes," I said, my open palm running down the front of her body and teasing her nipples to full erection. "I've been noticing that for weeks."

She moaned softly as I stroked her nipples gently. She squirmed slightly in her chair, and when I'd tormented her sufficiently for now I released her, coming around the side of the table and slowly screwing the corkscrew into the wine. I saw her eyes following the metal implement's entry into the resistant flesh of the cork with more than casual interest.

The sharp pop of the wine cork made her jump a little even though she was expecting it. I splashed wine into the glass and held it for her to sniff.

She did, and accepted the taste when I placed the smooth glass to her lips and tipped it.

"Excellent," she said.

"Very good, Ma'am," I told her, and poured a full glass of wine. Her eyes lingered over it and I allowed her another tiny sip, going slow so as not to soil that perfect dress, before disappearing into the kitchen.

Her lips, glossed red with wine, parted slightly as her eyes devoured the bowl of soup I set before her.

"Carrot-ginger curry," I said. "Soup of the day. Did you know that ginger is reputed to be an aphrodisiac?"

"You don't say," she muttered, squirming slightly as she tested the strength of the handcuffs, the chair, her wrists.

"Yes. Furthermore, one Dr. Kellogg, who not incidentally invented the corn flake, thought spicy food like curry encouraged impure thoughts."

"Did he?" she murmured, looking perturbed.

"Yes," I said. "Let's find out if he was right."

I stood behind her, towering over her small form as I curved my arms around her and took up her soup spoon. I lifted a spoonful of bright orange soup to her lips, which she parted obediently for me. I blew on the soup to cool it, then slipped the tip of the spoon between her wine-red lips. She slurped appreciatively.

"Too hot?" I asked her.

"Spicy," she said. "But not hot."

"Story of my life," I told Iris, and gave her another liquid spoonful. I fed her the soup with my arms coiled around her, feeling the warmth of her body as the spicy soup raised her skin temperature and made sweat break out on her flesh. Still, she ate all her soup like a good little diner. I punctuated every few spoonfuls with a sip of red wine. With each shift of my arms, I could feel her wriggling in my grasp.

"Was the soup to your liking, Ma'am?"

"Delicious," she said breathlessly, her mouth obviously hot from the curry.

I poured water from the clear pitcher and lifted the

23

glass to her lips. She dribbled a bit and I licked the droplets from her chin. She moaned softly and parted her lips for a kiss that never came.

I slipped away and glanced back to see her bare shoulders shivering as I went into the kitchen.

When I returned I held a tiny dish, no bigger than a shot glass, filled with a brightly coloured sorbet, arrayed on a small tray with a minuscule spoon.

"Passion fruit," I said. "A palate cleanser."

"Passion fruit?"

"Passion fruit."

I once again leaned over her, feeding her tiny nibbles of the sorbet from the very tip of the spoon. She sucked the confection into her mouth and swallowed greedily.

"Time for the next course," I told her without letting her finish the sorbet. She pouted noticeably and I leaned close to kissed those sorbet-shimmering lips, then pulled away at the last moment.

When I returned, I brought her appetizer. Oysters in fennel-cream sauce.

"Don't tell me," she whispered as I leaned close. "Fennel's an …"

"Aphrodisiac," I said with a cruel smile. "Reputedly, at least. You learn quickly, Ma'am. Open up."

I fed her each succulent oyster on the end of my best silver fork, teasing her lips gently and making her lean forward to get it. I could feel her heat rising, especially when her nipping teeth dislodged an oyster from the silver fork and made it fall to the chair between her slightly parted thighs.

"Ooops," I said, and dropped my hand between then, seizing the oyster. My hands lingered on the insides of her thighs, and I could feel her breath arrested as she waited for me to touch her. I did not, and tucked the sullied oyster into my apron pocket.

I could see her pouting noticeably as I took away the empty plate. She'd finished all her oysters, like a good girl.

I returned with another sorbet – mango.

"I've always thought mango tastes suspiciously like …"

"Don't say it," she whispered, her lips parting.

This time I let her have the whole tiny scoop of sorbet, and she moaned softly as its sweetness cooled her mouth. When I left her lips were glossed bright orange and the sips of wine she sucked at greedily – so greedily that droplets ran down her chin and onto her clothing.

"You've soiled this dress," I said.

"Oh," she whispered. "I guess I should run cold water through it."

"Yes," I told her. "I guess you should."

I unfastened her handcuffs and led her to the bathroom. I prepared the next course while I listened to the water running. When she emerged, I saw her face and cleavage were flushed, the latter made even more evident by the fact that she'd stripped off the dress and was now wearing only a white lace demi-bra and panties, white garter belt and white stockings.

I drew her hand to my face and licked her fingers. Under the clean tang of soap I could taste her. I pushed her against the wall, feeling her melt into my grasp.

"Did you make yourself come?" I asked.

She shook her head. "Mmm-uh," she mumbled, almost sadly.

"Good," I told her.

I handcuffed her to the chair again and this time her squirming was even more adorable. She'd wore a very skimpy thong, and I knew the wooden chair must be cold on her buttocks. Her nipples, hard and pink, had begun to poke out over the lace tops of her bra cups.

I brought out the main course: sautéed salmon and eggplant with coconut sauce.

"Eggplant I know about," she said softly. "But is coconut an aphrodisiac?"

"No," I said. "They just look like a pair of really big balls."

I fed her each morsel without care to neatness; coconut sauce ran down her chin and onto the swell of her cleavage. I felt her squirming against me as I leaned heavily against her shoulders. After the third bite I abandoned the fork and plucked pieces of salmon and eggplant with my fingers, making her lean forward to get them and teasing her lips open with my fingers before letting my fingertips remain behind, stroking her tongue as she swallowed. Soon my hand and her face were both covered, shimmering and savoury. I pressed my lips to hers and she once again melted into me, this time irrevocably, as my cock had begun to press so firmly against my apron that I knew I could stand no more.

"Fuck me," she begged. "Please don't make me wait."

My plans were decimated – I couldn't wait for dessert. I seized the key from my apron and undid one wrist of her handcuffs; she leapt from the chair and pushed herself against me before I could undo the other cuff, leaving the cuffs dangling half-open from her wrist. Her arms around me pulled me tight, and when I shoved her onto the table, neither of us hesitated or started at the sound of shattering china as we swept it to the floor.

I knocked the candles out of the way just in time to avoid setting her hair on fire. Glancing behind her, I was relieved to see they'd gone out as they tumbled. I was glad, now, that I'd spent the money on that sturdy dining room table. I climbed on top of her, her thighs opening in a succulent V as she clawed at my apron, lifting it, and groped after my cock in my dress slacks. I knelt over her as she eagerly undid my pants and took my cock into her mouth, her lips and tongue still warm from the oysters. She whimpered as her head bobbed up and down on me.

I guided her onto her back, slipped my body between her legs, her thighs closed tight around my hips. Pulling her thong to one side, I entered her, bringing a shudder to her body. I fucked her there on the table, slowly at first and then harder, course after course of deep thrusts into her, and when she came she clutched me so tight I couldn't resist it. I came inside her, my lips locked to hers, tasting oysters.

We had our dessert, after a fashion, sprawled in bed leaving stains everywhere. Who had the time to dab spilled wine and food from a body as luscious as that? I used my tongue, instead, and cleanliness was not my first concern.

It's a tragedy, really. All that time spent whipping the chocolate mousse, preparing the violet sauce to drizzle in a suggestive snakelike S atop the firm skin of the chilled dessert. It's really a shame, all those aphrodisiacs in one dessert and she didn't even get to enjoy it … because she was too busy being fucked.

But now it's the morning, and she's sleeping contentedly, her breasts still rose-colored with crystallized red wine and her lips moist with other, more savoury, liquors.

And morning's the best time for dessert.

Naked, I retrieved my apron and tied it around my body. I could feel my cock, wet with Iris's juices, rubbing against the rough cotton. The front of the apron was filthy, but isn't that what an apron's for? Ironically enough, this one didn't stop me from getting dirty last night.

I put the mousse on a tray and arranged it with a single violet blossom. I could hear her sighing softly as I entered the bedroom.

Spanish Olive
by Julia Price

"And this," said Armando, "Is where we mill the fruits."

Heather couldn't take her eyes off him. His long black hair belied his Spanish heritage, and the faint streams of grey just barely discernible in it gave him that look of distinction that always enticed Heather. His features were strong, an Iberian jaw and that powerful Roman nose – or was it a Madrid nose in this case? – which always drove Heather absolutely insane. And farming olives in the Sonoma sun had not only tanned him until his skin shone a rich olive colour itself; it had conditioned him until the shape of his body, muscled and gorgeous, was evident under the white oxford shirt he wore, even buttoned up as it was with a rep tie.

And he wore jeans. Jeans with a tie always turned Heather on. A throwback to her '80s childhood.

She'd come here to do a story for *The Daily* on Catherine Flanagan, a long-time Daily newspaper columnist who had retired and moved up to Sonoma to farm Spanish olives, her long-time passion. Ms Flanagan had hired Armando Flores, the foremost authority on Spanish olives. Heather had just heard in the informational video he'd shown her that Armando had been responsible almost single-handedly revitalizing the industry of gourmet olive oil production in Spain during the 1980s. Previously, Spanish olive oil had been considered inferior to Italian. Now, there was a strong cottage industry in gourmet olives and olive oil from Spain.

The 1980s? That meant he had to be at least 40. God, he could be 30. Oh my God, he's looking at me, thought Heather. She blushed and looked down, feeling her nipples stiffen behind her plain navy-blue suit.

"I'm sorry," said Armando. "I'm going into too much technical detail about the machines. Of course you're mostly interested in the fruit."

In fact, she had not heard a word he said. She had been entranced by the rhythm of his words, the timbre of his accent, the shape of his body and the scent of it. He had been telling her how olive oil was extracted from olives mechanically without chemicals, and she'd totally ignored him, choosing instead to focus on that lilting voice, those broad shoulders, that waist and the firm cheeks underneath, imprisoned in their tight jeans. She would have to go on the web later and figure out what the hell he had been talking about.

"Yes," said Heather breathlessly. "I'm incredibly interested in the fruit."

Armando smiled at her. "As any lady of discerning taste would be."

Heather blushed fiercely and looked down. Just as Armando had blushed when she'd asked him about the claim that he single-handedly revived gourmet olive oil production in Spain. "Perhaps they've overstated it," he had said, his boyish charm captivating her as he shyly explained that there had always been gourmet Spanish olives. "Perhaps I just helped popularized them a little bit," he said. "Just a little bit."

"Then I'll explain to you about the fruit," said Armando, his voice rich with his Spanish accent. "Please," he said. "Come with me."

Heather would have gone anywhere with Armando. She followed him through the long winding corridors of the ranch house, her eyes flickering from his shoulders to his back to his buns. God, he was gorgeous. It was the off-season and the ranch house was empty.

"That must be difficult, spending half the year in California and half the year in Spain," said Heather. "That must be very hard on your wife."

"Oh, I have no wife," said Armando.

"Ohhhh," Heather said softly. "That's too bad."

"Isn't it?" said Armando devilishly, turning to flash those gorgeous white teeth at her. Heather saw more than a hint of flirtation in his eyes, and she felt her body responding even as her mind rebelled. *Never fuck the interviewee*, her mentor, Sarah Laymon, had told her during one night drinking in the bar opposite the Daily's offices. *Never ever, ever, ever, ever fuck the interviewee*, she'd slurred, *Unless he's really, really, really cute and/or European. And if he's both, then definitely fuck him*. She'd burst into drunken laughter and sworn that she was kidding.

Armando led Heather into a luxurious tasting room filled with antiques and rich woods covered with velvet. He sat her down on an antique sofa and placed a tray in front of her.

On the tray were several small bowls of olives and several shot-glass sized containers of oil, plus some sprigs of mint and a glass of water.

"Please, clean your palate," said Armando, handing her a sprig.

31

She accepted it and chewed nervously. She swallowed and sipped water.

"Now," said Armando. "Close your eyes."

Heather almost passed out.

She closed her eyes and opened her mouth without being asked.

Armando placed an olive on her tongue.

"Chew it slowly," he said. "Savour it."

Heather did as she was told, feeling the salty, musky taste awaken her senses. It was awakening and enticing her so much, in fact, that she felt her nipples stiffen. Or perhaps it was the proximity of Armando, who was leaning very close to her, talking endlessly about the various attributes of the olive she'd just tasted.

"Now," he said. "Here's one from a different region."

This one was muskier and spicier, but didn't taste as salty. This time Armando's fingers lingered just a bit too long and Heather nipped them with her lips. The touch was electric.

"Can you taste it?" he smiled at her. "Can you taste Spain?" It was too good to pass up.

"Not yet," she said, and leaned forward and kissed him.

Armando didn't pull back. His hand came up behind her head and held her close as his tongue slipped into her mouth, kissing her deeply. Heather was already pulling off her jacket.

The tie was the hardest part, but once it was on the floor the shirt came open easily, even if the buttons did rattle annoyingly across the hardwood floor. Heather pushed Armando down onto the sofa and pressed her cheek to the soft fur of his bare chest. She inhaled deeply, smelling the rich aroma of recent sweat. Armando's fingers were running through her hair. She slid off the sofa and grabbed for Armando's belt.

I shouldn't be doing this, thought Heather, hesitating. *Even if he is cute and European.*

Then, "Fuck it," she said out loud, and pulled at Armando's belt.

His cock was good-sized and thick. She took it into her mouth and heard him moaning softly with a hint of that Spanish lilt. It had been so long since she'd had sex that Heather was afraid she wouldn't remember what to do, but it all came back to her as her lips worked up and down on Armando's cock. God, she wanted to fuck him. She reached under her skirt and pulled down her panties, climbing back on top of him.

"Wait," he said. "Lay on your back. Close your eyes."

"What?" Heather could feel her sex pulsing, hungry for him.

"Close your eyes," said Armando, reaching for the tray.

Heather closed her eyes and opened her mouth. He placed another olive on her tongue and she moaned softly as she chewed the musky salt, her moans growing louder as Armando pulled open her blouse and tugged down the lace of her bra cups. His mouth found her nipple and Heather's back arched as she swallowed the olive pulp. Her eyes still closed, she swirled in darkness as Armando's lips and tongue caressed her nipple.

"Is this an expensive bra?" he asked.

"No, not really."

"Good," he said, and Heather gasped as she felt the cold dribble of olive oil on her breasts. Armando undid the front clasp of her bra and pulled it open, smearing the olive oil everywhere with her tongue.

But it's an expensive blouse, thought Heather. suddenly not caring. she struggled out of her blouse ?

kicked off her high-heeled shoes as Armando quickly stood up and pulled off his jeans and boots. He helped her out of her skirt and Heather lay there on the velvet sofa wearing nothing but her panties.

Armando looked down at her, his dark eyes flashing as he took in her slim form. Then he reached out and grabbed the small carafe of olive oil, plucking the stopper from it and upending it over her.

"The antiques?" Heather asked breathlessly.

"Fuck it," said Armando, and poured olive oil onto her.

Her breasts were soon coated with the stuff, and he let the thin stream make its way down her belly to her sex. Heather slipped off her panties and spread her legs, and Armando's olive oil oozed down between her lips, coating her sex.

When he slid on top of her there was a divine feeling of slipperiness, their bodies sliding together so smoothly that there was almost no friction. Armando was really an olive oil connoisseur; after licking hungrily at heather's oil-coated lips, his tongue trailed its way down over her breasts and belly and he knelt on the floor, his face finding its way between her oil-slick thighs.

"Oh God," moaned Heather.

Armando's tongue slipped between her lips and found her clit almost immediately. The oil lent it an extra smoothness, and her eyes went wide as he worked on her clit. His hands came up, roving over her slick breasts, pinching her slippery nipples, moving up to her mouth so she could lick the oil from his fingers. It tasted buttery, seductive, soft. Armando came up from between her thighs, his cock hard and ready for her.

"Wait," she said, and reached for the carafe.

She poured oil onto his cock, coating it. She stroked it

with her hand, a little surprised at how large it felt. It had been so long since she had sex, she didn't want to take any chances, even as wet as she was.

And as she guided Armando's oil-smooth cock into her, the feeling of it going into her was divine.

Heather moaned uncontrollably as Armando slid into her, the oil providing an extra heightening of sensation. He rested heavily atop her, kissing her deeply, his hips moving smoothly as he fucked her. Heather's hand moved down his back and cupped those divine buns, her fingers slippery with oil as she sought purchase. she finally gave up and lay there with her hands inert, letting Armando do all the work, which he seemed more than capable of doing. His cock, so thick, was hitting just the right spot, and as he licked down and suckled on her olive-oil nipple, she knew she was going to come.

"Please," she begged him. "Come inside me."

His oiled-up cock pumped rapidly inside her as he sought his orgasm, and it was the merciless thrusting as he tried to come that made Heather come herself. Her orgasm was intense, her muscles clenching around the thrusting shaft of Armando's cock as he groaned, fucked her faster, and came inside her, his come mingling with the oil.

When he'd climaxed, he slid to a rest on top of her, their bodies still slick. His cock remained in her, half-hard, for long minutes. Then it slipped out, and Heather could feel the faint dribble of fluid coming out – Armando mixed with the oil.

"It's not really an antique," he said, looking down at the oil-soaked sofa.

"Like I care," answered Heather.

She reached out to the tray, seized an olive, and popped it into Armando's mouth. He chewed and kisse her. She tasted salt.

Never fuck an interviewee, she remembered Sarah telling her one time when they were both so drunk she'd forgotten it until now. *Unless he's an olive oil salesman.* Then she'd started giggling uncontrollably, as if she was remembering something truly wicked, but had refused to tell Heather what she was laughing about.

Heather looked up suspiciously at Armando, then sighed.

"You're a hell of an olive oil salesman," she said.

"This olive oil sells itself," smiled Armando, running his hand over Heather's shiny breast.

Amy's Tattoo
by Shanna Germain

Ingredients:
  1/2 oz. dark rum
  1/2 oz. white rum
  2 oz. pineapple juice
  2 oz. orange juice
  Splash of grenadine

Directions:
  On a hot summer day, fill a tall frosted glass with ice, pour in run and juice. Float the grenadine over the top. Sit back and sip – works almost as well as a cold shower.

I want to lick it. I can't help it.

It's partially the colour – that deep red, almost crimson, darker than any real strawberry would ever be – pinpricked into the pale skin of your lower back. It's partially the excitement of seeing it for the first time, its beautiful round shape peeking out from beneath your white bikini as you lay in the backyard.

I catch my first glimpse of it from the living room window, where I'm watering the plants – pretending to water the plants – when instead I'm watching you. I've

37

already pulled on my swimsuit and grabbed a book, ready to join you in the back yard for some summer sun, but now I'm stilled, stopped by the sight before me, unable to break away. I know you can't see me through the window, but holding the watering can gives me an excuse to dawdle in front of the glass and savour the sight of you for a few minutes longer.

You shift on the blanket, pull down your bikini bottom a little further in search of a lower tan line, and there it is: green crown, red berry glistening like a real piece of fruit, just asking to be fingered and plucked, sucked and swallowed. It's almost enough to make me forget your lean runner's legs, your bare back, the bright red braids that fall over the pages of your book. It's almost enough to make me forget our vow – that we'd live together only as friends and roommates, that we would never ruin our five-year friendship by admitting there was something more.

I can't believe in all these years that I've never seen it. You must keep it well hidden beneath the sweaters and long shirts you wear – is this on purpose, I wonder? Do you know what it will do to me?

I hold the watering can at an angle, pretend I am concentrating deeply on the moisture needs of the philodendron and feel my tongue start to ache inside my mouth. I imagine bending over you in the yard, running my tongue across the tattoo, feeling the bumps in your skin as though they are strawberry seeds, sucking your sweet flesh into my mouth. The bold red colour matches your hair, makes your pale skin glow in contrast. I wonder if it's the same colour as your nipples, if they stand out like raspberries against your chest when they're hard.

I imagine being the one holding the needle while you

lay in a chair, unable to see me, and let me press the colours and pain into your skin. You must trust me, I say, pressing my palm against your back to hold you steady, and you acquiesce, but I can feel the fear buzzing across your skin. I imagine you squirming just a little, trying to pretend that it doesn't hurt, that you don't feel the pain, that you're really getting a tattoo for the way it looks and not the way it makes you feel. Why the small of the back then? That one place where the pain is so intense that it makes your spine tingle with need. I know – I have one there too, but you've never seen it. It's older than yours, a little more faded, a little softer around the edges. It says something, but I won't tell you what, only that it's waiting for someone to covet it, to run their fingers along it as though they're reading erotica in Braille.

My cheeks feel flushed, and I tell myself it's just from standing too close to the window, but I know that's not the truth. Your head is down on your hands now, the book is closed, and I wonder if you're sleeping or just daydreaming. Are you imagining us together? Do you ever wonder what it would be like if, just one time, you reached across the couch while we were watching a movie? Or if we allowed those casual bumps in the hallway to linger, stop, stretch out until our fingers were fumbling and pulling and stroking against skin? Do you ever, as I do, lay in bed at night, whispering your fingers between your legs, saying a name over and over so quietly, so softly, that no one but you can hear it?

I watch as you stir a little and crack your legs open just slightly. The sun is high in the sky and I imagine you're sweating, baby beads of moisture collecting on your tattoo like dew. If I were to lay my tongue against it, it would taste salty and sweet, more oyster than fruit. Just the way I imagine your pink lips would taste in my

39

mouth, if I sucked your sweet juices until you were dry, until you were crying for me to stop, begging me not to. The skin beneath your tattoo would be sun-warmed, juicy, ready for me, perfectly ripe, perfectly ready to be grasped with two fingers and pulled into my mouth. It makes me want to run my finger up your spine, find out where the soft fruit ends and the hardness of your bones begin, to find out what I can crush and what will crush me in return.

I set the watering can down and run my hands down my stomach. Are you sleeping, I wonder, as I slip my hand into my bikini bottom, ready to blow it all if I have to, ready to lose our friendship, because I can't sit here and watch anymore without touching myself, without at least pretending that my tongue is tracing the red fruit, tasting your flesh. I'm so wet that I don't even need any lubricant – I just slide my fingers against my own pink flesh and rub, pretending that it's your hand, that my own hands are squeezing your raspberry nipples, that when you're done touching me I'll be able to turn you over, lay you down on your stomach, finally taste the flesh beneath the tattoo. Just the thought of it makes me so hot I can barely stand up, and lean my head against the window and close my eyes. I keep rubbing, praying that you're not looking up, but hoping that you are, because I can't stop myself, I don't want to stop myself. The taste of strawberries fills my mouth and then I'm coming, trying not to bang my head against the glass as beams of pleasure shine through me.

I take a few deep breaths, then open my eyes to see you lying just as you were before, your head resting on one bent arm. But just as I step away from the window, I see you reach back and flick your suit down, just enough so that it uncovers the very bottom of your tattoo. The gentle curve of the fruit, the way it points down and to the middle, as though it's an arrow or invitation. Then you look over your shoulder and smile, and I realize that you meant for me to see it all along.

Seven Courses
by N.T. Morley

You've been laid out nude on a wheeled wooden table. Your wrists and ankles have been shackled to the corners of the table. Your legs are spread very wide. Your thighs and knees are strapped down similarly. Your waist is belted as well, fixed tight with a leather strap; another strap goes under your breasts and a third above them, affixed to the table under your armpits so that not even the slightest movement of your torso is possible. Your collar has been ratcheted very tight to the table, so you cannot move your head.

Your vagina, opened wide with a tasteful metal device, has been filled with thin-sliced pears arranged like a flower. You can feel their cool stickiness against your smooth-shaved vaginal lips. There is more stickiness and coolness deep inside you, where you have been filled with cherries. Your anus, however, has been spared being used as a fruit dish; it has, instead, been filled with a thick, exceedingly deep plug that has been attached to the table, to keep you quite still. You would be quite unable to dislodge it, even if the straps were released, which of course they will not be. But it does remind you of your inability to move, and the way it presses against your filled pussy from inside is a further sensation to remind you what will happen when the pear slices have been exhausted and the hungry guests go after the cherries.

Across your smooth pubis are strawberry wedges. On your flat belly are artfully arranged chocolate-covered mandarin orange slices. Your breasts are hidden by pineapple chunks skewered by toothpicks. Your hair has been braided in such a way that it holds its many cherries by the stem. Your forehead and your arms are covered with peach halves. Your legs hold sugared lemon slices. Between your freshly scrubbed toes have been placed apricot segments.

Your memories of the preparation ritual are dim. They are lost in the pulse and heat of your arousal, because the caterers who prepared you took great care to caress your genitals and nipples every few minutes. They also punctuated their caresses with full-mouthed kisses, and now your whole body feels alive with sexual arousal.

The shaving, also, was unexpectedly arousing for you. You have never been shaved by another person before. Especially not down there. You are now smooth and scrubbed and pink in your bondage, the perfect repository for the succulent victuals the banquet guests demand.

You have also not been fed for many hours; the weak feeling deep in your stomach mingles with the overwhelming smell of fruit all around you to make you ache throughout your naked body. The hunger becomes one with the arousal. Your stomach and your pussy are one.

Affixed to your clitoral ring is a single white dwarf daisy – the perfect garnish for the perfect assortment.

You are wheeled into the reception hall. You smell the

scents of expensive wine and liquor, cigars, $1,000-an-ounce perfume. A faint cheer goes up as you are wheeled into the centre of the room. The guests converge on you, and you feel your immobile body being touched all over.

The pear slices go first, perhaps because the guests want to touch your pussy. Then someone starts grabbing pineapple slices, carelessly poking your breasts with the toothpicks as they do. Pineapple juice coats your breasts, running down into your armpits. Once the pear slices in your pussy are gone, you feel fingers invading you as they seek after the cherries. Your pussy feels so full to begin with, stuffed with fruit, but as more than one hand searches inside you at once, the pressure against your sensitized vaginal walls overwhelms you. You begin to shudder. But you cannot move, not even enough to upset the banquet.

The cherries have been de-stemmed. Fingers seek deep inside you, plucking the slippery orbs. Meanwhile, you see a face above you as a woman squeezes orange slices into your open mouth. You drink the succulent juice drop by drop. A cherry-seeker gets the bright idea of unlatching the speculum; you feel it sliding out and you moan as your pussy closes tightly around the cherries. You have been opened so wide by the speculum, lubricated so efficiently by the caterers, that it is an easy matter for the petite woman to thrust her whole hand inside you, making your eyes go wide and a choking gasp come deep in your throat. Someone strokes your forehead, which is still sticky. The woman presses deep and you feel the throb of your clitoris. Someone else has bent low and is suckling the pineapple juice from your nipples. The woman takes her time finding the cherries lost in your pussy; you feel the heel of her hand pressing up against your G-spot and suddenly you're getting close – very close. You throb on the edge of orgasm as the woman brings her small hand out cupping a treasure trove of half-crushed cherries, leaking succulent juice down her wrist. She smears the partially mashed fruit over your pussy and pubic region; other guests reach for them, scooping up the cherries that have remained mostly whole. Within moments there is nothing more than a mashed cherry pulp leaking down your vaginal lips, coating your aching, throbbing clitoris.

Someone, perhaps desperately hungry, climbs onto the table between your spread thighs and bends forward to lick the cherry juice and mash off of your clitoris.

You wail deep in your throat, as her tongue trails up your clitoris. The woman with the small hands has positioned herself beside the one licking your clit, and a third and fourth are savouring the taste of pineapple from your nipples. You feel the small hand sliding into you again, this time no longer seeking after cherries. You feel yourself filled again, this time with an intentionality that makes tears stand out in your eyes. The woman's mouth closes on your clitoris. Someone, a fifth person, bends low over your face with a sugared lemon slice in his or her mouth. You taste the sweet lemon and the stranger's tongue at the same moment your orgasm explodes through you.

The shudder and squirm of your body shakes the few remaining morsels from your skin. You can feel the thick plug in your anus, holding you still, and as your muscles tighten that plug makes you gasp, as if it's being thrust still deeper inside you. Your climax makes the room seem to spin, and you hear yourself moaning, loudly, desperately, your jaw aching, your throat thick with juice. More people are kissing you. Each mouth has a piece of fruit in it. New people move to your sex, others

45

savouring your nipples. A mouth on your clit. Another small hand in your pussy. Another mouth against yours, feeding you as you whimper and come again. And again. And again. The sweet taste of fruit filling your mouth and throat as pressure builds in your cunt, then releases in an explosion of surrender. You feel a cock in your mouth, and the salt taste of come complements the sweetness of fruit.

There is no main course: In this banquet, you are all seven courses. Within hours you are nothing more than a limp dessert, a nude body covered with the sticky remains of fruit, your own sex and the come and juices of others. The guests have savoured their after-dinner drinks and cigars. They have dressed and departed.

You feel the presence of the caterers, above you, caressing your nipples, sex and face as they did earlier, when they were preparing you. You taste their kisses. You feel their fingers inside you, checking to make sure nothing has been left behind. They wheel the table out of the banquet hall and into the kitchen. You feel the spray of warm water, the scrub of soapy sponges. You feel your arousal mounting again as they scrub the sugary juice from your sex. You come a fifth or sixth or perhaps seventh time as they fill your pussy with warm water, flushing it, and ease the plug out of your anus. You remain limp as they unfasten your restraints, roll you over, unbraid your hair. They lift you off of the table and set you down on a large plastic frame. You feel yourself sliding into the warmth of a closed space, hear the door closing behind you. There is a loud hum all around you.

As you shift, you hear the clanking of crockery.

You're being washed with the rest of the dishes.

The hot jets of water hit your naked body, and when they linger over your cunt you come again.

Menthol Attack
by Benedict Green

Lolling in and out of consciousness, I saw a vision of the Angel of Death. She had a hot little camisole on, tight around her slim, perky breasts, and a black garter belt with lace-top seamed stockings. A black lace G-string with a string of little red hearts completed the ensemble.

"What do you think?" she asked me. "Too slutty?"

I popped another cherry-flavoured cough drop and looked her up and down. She looked good in that outfit, and if I hadn't been staring into the vast abyss of eternal darkness, she would have given me quite a hard-on. I sucked on the sticky sweet of the cough drop and stifled a pulmonary eruption as I tried to speak.

"I don't know," I rasped. "It's pretty slutty."

"But is it *too* slutty?"

I reached out and grabbed Melanie, then pulled her onto the bed, tumbling her over the mound of covers piled atop me. Her pretty white bum gestured up to me invitingly and I swatted it, right where the arrow plunged through the Irish-red heart. She yelped and swatted me back, lightly, on the arm.

"That's not playing fair," Melanie said. "I can't hit you back, because you're sick."

I spanked her again and squirmed, reaching back and grabbing my wrist. "Stop it!" she barked. "Tell me if I look too slutty!"

"I'm giving you your answer," I said, wrenching my hand free from her grasp and preparing to spank her again. She got a stern look on her face, eyes wide, lips pursed, and I relented. Stifling another cough as I sucked on the cherry drop, I ran my fingertips lightly over her smooth ass, loving the way the G-string crept tight and tiny up between her cheeks. I eased my hand between her slightly parted cheeks and began to rub her pussy.

Mel sighed gently. "That sounds like a yes," she said, arching her back and pushing her butt up into my grasp. She was wet, and when I tucked my fingers under the none-too-substantial crotch of the G-string, she wriggled alluringly and pushed herself more firmly onto my hand.

"Definitely slutty," I said. "I wish I was well enough to really do something about it." I covered my mouth and coughed, and she rolled over, straddling me and pushing her tits into my face.

"You're evil," she growled. "Getting me all turned the fuck on and then claiming illness. Have you been taking the herbs I gave you?"

I bent forward and nipped at her breasts. She plucked them away, swaying just out of reach. "Martin! Did you take my fucking herbs?"

"Yes, well, about those —"

"And the herbal syrup?"

"Well, it tastes kind of —"

"And the cough drops?" Now she was getting pissed.

"I'm sticking to cherry."

"Pervert! I gave you the herbal ones."

I coughed. "They're too strong."

"They're menthol-fucking-ated," she growled.

48

"They make my mouth hurt."

"They're supposed to make your mouth hurt," she said severely. "They also numb your throat. You are the *worst* sick person I have ever dated."

I shrugged.

"You won't even feel me up properly," she said, clamping her thighs around me and humping me playfully. "You get me all wet and then next thing you know you're too sick. And I go to the trouble of trying on lingerie for you and everything."

"All right," I said. "I'm a bad sick person. Better than being a bad well person."

"If you'd use my magic herbal cough drops, you'd be better by now."

"No."

"Just try one."

"They hurt."

She got that look in her eyes, smiled slightly. She leaned close, her tits brushing my chest. She began to nuzzle my throat. She kissed her way up my chin and pressed her lips to mine, her tongue wriggling its way into my mouth as she ground her pelvis firmly against my crotch. Even through the pile of blankets, I could feel its heat. Deftly, Melanie sucked the cherry-flavoured cough drop out of my mouth and spat it across the room.

"Bitch," I said, grabbing her sides and tickling her.

Melanie is impossible to tickle. She slapped my shoulders and bounced up and down. "That's the spirit! Fighting spirit! Cough drop! Try the cough drop!"

"God damn it," I said. "You're the stubbornest –"

"Most stubborn," she said, grabbing the environmentally friendly wax paper package from the nightstand and tearing it open. She plucked out a brown lozenge. "Try it."

Grimly, I opened my mouth.

She popped it in and my mouth was enveloped in a taste sensation at once sickly sweet and nauseatingly icy cool. Flushes of heat went through my face.

"Yuck," I said, and opened my mouth wide, sticking out my tongue with the lozenge resting defiantly on it.

Melanie sighed. "Only one thing to try, then," she said, and plucked the cough drop off my tongue. Before I knew it, she'd popped it in her own mouth, peeled back the covers, and was burrowing her way underneath, slutty lingerie and all.

"What are you doing?" I asked suspiciously.

If there's one thing Melanie knows, it's how to get my drawstring sweat pants untied quickly. Pushing them down around my knees, she took my cock in her hand. It was already half-hard from my feisty girlfriend's insistence on jocular banter. When her mouth moulded to it, the sizzle/chill of mentholated goodness overwhelmed it, and it was hard all the way in an instant.

"Holy fuck," I said. "Stop that!"

Her mouth lifted off my cock for a split second. "I can't hear you," she called out, her voice muffled by about ten pounds of blankets and her syllables punctuated by the soft clack of the lozenge against her teeth. My whole body shivered as the pastille from hell swirled up and down the shaft of my cock, teased into motion by Mel's adroit tongue. I gasped when she tickled the very tip of my cock, salving the sensitive glans with the icy hot sensation.

"Stop that!" I said, but by then I was so hard Mel wouldn't have listened to me even if my hips hadn't been slowly circling in time with her ministrations. Once Mel gets started sucking cock, there's only one thing that can stop her.

50

I was all the way in her mouth, now, the full length of my shaft enveloped by the warmth of her mouth and the shimmering sensations of heat and cold. I moaned, lifting my hips high as Mel's hands reached under to grip my ass-cheeks. She was sucking me rhythmically, the way she does it when she wants me to come. I felt numb, though, my cock surrounded by bizarre sensations that left me unsure of where I was.

Mel found where I was, her mouth coming up and sucking tightly around my head, the lozenge pressed to the tip of my cock as she stroked me with her hand.

"Fuck," I gasped. "I'm going to –"

I learned right then that there's a curious sensation that comes with an orgasm had in the midst of a menthol attack. It's like the surface sensations of penile stimulation overtake the deep burst of pleasure that forms a climax, and my whole body went cold then hot in an instant. Mel stayed with me, her full, tight lips tight around my cock as I came in her mouth, moaning.

She sat up, sweeping the heavy covers back, munching conspicuously.

"Yum yum yum," she said. "Minty fresh come." She swallowed. And smiled like the cat who ate the canary.

"Are you happy now?"

"Mmm-hmmm," she grinned. "I got you to try it. Do you feel better?"

"Much," I said. I yanked the covers back over her head and reached out for my cherry drops

All-Day Sucker
by Jacqueline Pinchot

Emma had a taste for candy. She couldn't make it through the day without a chocolate bar, a handful of gumdrops, or a rope of liquorice. Sometimes she ate much more than a few of her chosen treats, working her way through a heart-shaped box of See's or a row of jelly donuts. Luckily, she'd been blessed with a dream metabolism, one that was always ready to burn up whatever she devoured.

At work, they called her "sugar roll," "sweet-tart," or "lollypop," depending on what mouth-watering snack she brought in to share. She didn't mind the nicknames, as they described the rest of her looks, as well. She *was* sweet, with cotton candy pink lips and black cherry curls and eyes the exact same hue as dark molasses. She *dressed* sweet, in candy colours, peppermint-stick-striped sweaters, suits in the rich, jewel tones of hard candy, skirts and tops the exact juicy red of a glazed candy apple.

And, although the rest of her co-workers didn't know this, she *tasted* sweet. Her cunt reflected the flavours of her favourite candies, combining to make a nectar of cum that was like ambrosia, honey-scented, sugar-rich. All of her lovers had commented on her exotic flavour, her unique scent, and all, even long after their break-ups, had remembered the taste of her pussy with a wistful pleasure.

At night, when she made herself come, she would dip her fingers into her mouth afterwards and lick them clean. Her fragrant cum was as good as any candy she'd ever had. Her only regret was that she'd never met a woman with a cunt as divine, as rich as her own.

That is, until her new boss, Clarice, arrived. Emma liked this woman immediately. Clarice had incredible style. She wore her short blonde hair slicked back and it gleamed like some sort of glazed confection beneath the office's fluorescent lights. She dressed in more subdued tones than Emma, but her cashmere suits were in shades of warm, chocolate browns and she slicked her lips with the dark red hues you can only find when biting into a home-made cherry pie.

Emma was intrigued, at first, by her boss's appearance. But she found herself drawn even closer to something more subtle, more difficult to place. At meetings, Emma seated herself as close to Clarice as possible. In the elevator, she stood directly behind her new boss and breathed in deeply, trying to place the nameless fragrance tickling her nose. Until … until it came to her, in the middle of the night, that hard-to-place perfume. Something spicy, like a cup of apple cider. Something tangy, like fresh gingerbread, warm from the oven. Something sweet, like candy, like Emma's own honeyed cunt.

Emma decided to stay late the evening after her midnight revelation, knowing her boss was putting in extra hours to finish a big project. And, as Clarice took off her jacket, as her smell began to permeate the room,

Emma followed suit, loosening the top two buttons on her raspberry silk blouse, removing her blazer, undoing her dark cherry-pop curls from their staid French braids.

When they were finished working, Clarice settled back in her chair, looking pleased. Then she sighed, took a deep breath, and sighed again. Her eyes lit on Emma's, and held. Clarice knew it wasn't appropriate, what she was thinking, what she was wanting. But, seeing her own desire reflected in Emma's eyes, she decided to make a move. She stood and came to Emma's side, then bent and inhaled deeply. Emma lifted her face to her boss's, and said, "You're as sweet as I am, aren't you?"

Clarice shook her head, "Slightly spicier, I think. Or so I've been told ..."

"I'd like to taste for myself," Emma said softly. And that was all she needed to say. Emma was free of her candy-coloured outfit before Clarice had her clothing off. They spread themselves out, luxuriously, on the table and dined upon each other's cunts. Savouring the difference in their flavours, the bouquet of their cum, the lingering full-bodied aroma. Like connoisseurs of fine wines, they murmured descriptions to each other, "Warm and sweet ..."

"Rich and delicious ..."

"Like licking an all-day sucker."

That was Clarice's summation of Emma's cunt, and she couldn't get it out of her mind. Not even as her fingers joined in and probed Emma deeply. Not even as Emma, setting her own rhythm, locked her lips to Clarice's jewel and sucked and tickled and lapped like a kitten drinking from a saucer of warm milk. Clarice was captivated by the confection before her, the treat, like a magic bag on Halloween that never empties. Emma had the ability to come and come and come, each time producing more of the fragrant nectar that Clarice found herself drunk upon.

They were inseparable after that, after hours, of course. But office gossip picked up quickly. Especially after Clarice began bringing candy each day for Emma, leaving the lollipops wrapped in satin ribbons on her desk

Fuck-Me Fruits
by Xavier Acton

She's got these shoes, see. Or she *had* these shoes. Sandals, really. I don't know what it is about them. She wears them when she's sunning. She wears them when she's laying on the chaise lounge in the back yard, sheathed only in a white string bikini. And these glorious, unbelievable shoes.

They're trashy – she got them at some discount store when they'd been discounted 95% or something. They're tacky – she would probably never wear them in public, but she likes wearing them around the house. They're impractical – platform heeled thongs, white plastic, with a gaudy spray of grapes, crab apples, ivy leaves and berries tucked just above the single toe strap. But they match her string bikini perfectly – shameless, garish, skimpy, revealing, and cheap. And sexy enough to make my cock hard every time she puts them on.

I've never confessed it to her; how could I? She makes fun of them herself, calling them her "Fuck me Fruits." She wears them a lot, though; all summer long, she savours her sunbathing, stretching out on the chaise lounge and displaying her body in its twin infinitesimal white spandex prisons. I watch her, and I get hard as a rock.

This afternoon, I decided I couldn't take it any more. I was watching as she lay there in the sun, her eyes shrouded by dark glasses, her skin glistening with sweat in the sun, her nipples hard and showing through the bikini top. Her feet lay there, taunting, casually crossed at the end of the chaise lounge as she leafed through one of those women's magazines that consists mostly of underwear ads. Her hair was tied back in a fruit-print bandanna, and that was the last straw.

I watched her stretch in the sun, stifle a small yawn, toss the magazine on the patio and reach back to ratchet the chaise lounge into a flat position. She kicked off the fuck-me-fruits, rolled over onto her belly, and spread her legs. The string of her thong disappeared fetchingly between her cheeks, and the fuck-me-fruits taunted me without mercy.

I banged the screen door, but she didn't hear me.

She looked up as I approached her. "Hi, honey," she said, stifling another yawn. "What are you doing here?"

The shoes lay there, goading me, one upright, one casually turned on its side, their fruits shimmering plastic and moist in the sun. I seized the shoes and slapped the side of her legs.

"Roll over," I told her.

"Why?" she asked as she rolled over onto her butt, sitting up. I got up and went behind her, pulling the back of the chaise lounge into a reclining position. She leaned back onto it, looking confused.

"What are you doing?" she asked.

Reverently, I lifted first one of her delicate feet, then the other, sliding the thongs onto her. Her eyes were probably spinning with puzzlement behind those dark glasses, but I didn't care.

"These shoes have been begging to be devoured for too fucking long," I growled. "Today's the day they get what they want."

She giggled, as if she couldn't believe what was happening. My mouth descended to her feet and I began to trace the outline of the plastic fruit with my tongue. When I tickled her flesh, the sensitive, bony slope at the top of her feet, she gasped and giggled.

My hands crept up her thigh, and she didn't even move to slap my hand away when my fingertips plucked away the skimpy crotch of her bikini bottoms and tucked it to the side.

She did utter one faint protest: "What will the neighbours think," but she said it even as her legs were sliding further open. My fingers entered her, two of them, and I began finger fucking her as I licked her shoes. "Fuck," she moaned. "Fuck, that feels good."

I ran my tongue all over the fuck-me-fruits, consumed with hunger for them. I bit and gnawed at the plastic fruits as I fucked her cunt with two fingers, then three. She squirmed on the chaise lounge, gripping her thighs as her ass lifted off the plastic seat. I bit down hard on her fuck-me-fruits and ripped off a great globular grape, spitting it across the patio into the ivy.

She giggled, but her giggle turned in to a gasp when I curved my fingers up and pressed against her G-spot, my thumb finding her clit. I took another bite and spat a crab-apple into the pool. She moaned softly as I ripped a tender plastic ivy leaf and let it fall in glistening splendour to the plastic bands of the chaise lounge.

"Fuck," she moaned softly as I ripped at her shoes. "I'm going to come –" she whimpered and grasped her thighs, shuddering all over as I tore another mouthful of plastic fruit and launched it into the flower bed in a sputtering haze of saliva. She continued to come even as I shredded the last, pathetic grape that clung with desperation to the thin white strap of her sandals, like the terrified survivor of a frontier massacre.

Her quick breaths turning to slow, satisfied sighs, she looked down at me, no less puzzled than before, though my purpose had apparently, by now, been made clear to her.

"My fuck-me-fruits," she groaned sadly.

"It's all right," I told her. "I saw another pair for sale at the thrift store."

Juice For Breakfast
by Sage Vivant

Ray was a man who liked to reward one good deed with another. If that meant eating Terry out for breakfast, so be it. He owed her at least that after her fine fellatio the previous morning. She slept soundly now, but he grinned thinking about how she'd be squirming shortly.

She was a light sleeper – sudden movements would surely wake her. Her back was to him. She slept on her side, with her legs partially open like scissors that had been put down carelessly. With one hand on his insistent woody, he slipped the other between her legs, following her moist heat as his target.

The soft hair of her pussy tickled his curious fingers. Her top leg, drawn slightly upward toward her body, created the slimmest little crevice for him to explore. He landed lightly on the puffy softness that protected her slit. She didn't move.

With excruciating care, he stroked the small patch of cunt available to him. As he traced his finger over the same spot over and over, moisture slowly worked its way outward over her swelling labia. Her leg moved up, closer to her body, exposing more of her pussy.

He couldn't know whether she was awake but he did

know her pussy was primed. The urge to slide his finger up inside her consumed him. As he pushed into her, her wetness cloaked him with steamy permission.

His earlier concerns about waking her no longer seemed important. He let go of his rock-hard member and slid under the covers in one smooth motion, gently sweeping a palm over her ass cheek before he licked her butt cleavage. As he worked his way down with quicker, more furtive laps, he inhaled her intensely musky scent. He loved the way she smelled before she bathed in the morning.

He spread her swollen, slippery lips open with his thumbs and headed for her furry blond cunt without a moment's hesitation. She fidgeted languorously, smearing her juice on his nose and cheek.

He followed the length of her opening with his tongue, struggling somewhat to cover the area he intended to eat. The angle was suddenly awkward – or maybe his hunger for her was no longer content with such limited access.

She rolled over on her stomach and tucked in her knees to raise her ass up in the air. He positioned himself quickly between her legs and immediately dove into her muff. She pushed her dripping snatch into his eager face and he lapped at her wildly, savouring the taste of her as he burrowed deeper between her legs. He found her clit with his thumb and rubbed mercilessly. Meanwhile, he pressed his lips to her pussy hole, sending vibrations throughout her cunt. She gasped and ground her wet pussy into his face as he frigged her clit and licked her slit. She practically drenched his face with juice when she exploded with pleasure.

He returned to his pillow. "Oh, did I wake you?"

She exhaled deeply, eyes closed. A huge and seemingly permanent grin adorned her face.

Sugar Free
by Matthew Leland

I quit sugar. Cold turkey. Total detox. It's part of an overall regimen of trying to get healthy as I approach my thirties. But it's been a real bitch. Luckily, Kelly's a real bitch, too.

Don't get me wrong; I asked her to be a bitch. But she's a little better at it than I thought she would be.

"Listen, Kel," I told her. "You need to keep an eye on me. I can give up everything with sugar in it – except chocolate. You have to watch me. Don't let me slide on the chocolate issue."

Kelly's a health food nut, and she can't stand chocolate. Can you believe it? She's one of those weird freaks who was born without the chocolate gene. I've known three of them in my entire life. Three people who didn't like chocolate, and guess what? They're all total sex fiends.

And I know what you're going to ask. Yes, Kelly too. More than any of the others. More than any woman I've ever known. I think chocolate fails to have any appeal to her because all she thinks about is sex. Hand her a chocolate-covered Dove bar and she looks disappointed. Then she starts wondering if it'll cause a yeast infection if she fucks herself with it. She's not human, I swear.

It's been three weeks. When we go out to dinner and the dessert cart passes by, Kelly flashes her cleavage at me or gropes my crotch under the table. When we're in the park and my eyes linger on the snack stand with its terrifying array of candy bars, she grabs my hand, wraps my arm around her and shoves it down her shirt until the temptation is behind us.

"Just a little bite," I pleaded with her once as we walked past ice cream shop. "I'll just ask for a taste. Wouldn't that be better than holding out and then crashing later? Wouldn't it be better to get a taste now than to eat a whole scoop?"

She smiled, and beckoned me to lean down so she could whisper into my ear.

"How would you like to go the next year without blowjobs?"

"You wouldn't," I said.

"All right," she said. "You're not convinced. The next year without blowjobs, and the next three months without fucking."

"You *really* wouldn't," I said.

She shrugged. "You know how much I love you," she said.

"You couldn't stand it."

"You *asked* for the help, honey."

We walked past the ice cream store without stopping.

"I'm going to walk down to the store," I told her once, nervously, on a Saturday about 4:00.

She looked up from the book she was reading. She regarded me with eyes narrowed. "To get what?"

"We're out of paper towels."

She sighed, shook her head sadly and returned her attention to the book. "It's really a shame. I *so* used to enjoy giving you head. A whole year, honey – is it really worth it?"

She looked up at me again, a wicked smile on her face. She licked her lips.

"Is it?"

I never made it down to the store that day.

The last straw came when we were sitting on the couch watching a movie. She was wearing nothing but a pair of panties and a tight belly-baring T-shirt. She looked good and she smelled better, but I couldn't take my mind off of chocolate.

"I think I'm going to give up," I said.

She raised the remote control and hit PAUSE.

"Give up on the movie?"

"No," I said. "On chocolate."

"No blowjobs," she said.

"I'm not kidding," I told her. "I'm rescinding my offer for help. I can't take it."

She sighed.

"You really mean it? You're going to give in? You've been doing so well."

"I know," I said. "I can't take it. I'm going to go to the store."

Kelly shook her head and kissed me. "Look. Another hour and it'll be closed. You can make it."

"I can't," I said. "I'm sick of it."

"What if I sweetened the pot?"

"Don't give me that blowjob ultimatum," I said. "Really. I can't hold out any longer. Besides, I know you could never make good on that threat."

"Probably not," she said. "If you really want to give in, go ahead. It's your choice. But if you'll give me just one hour, I promise you'll make it another day."

"Sex won't do it," I told her.

"I'm not talking about sex," she said. "I'm talking about chocolate."

I looked at her suspiciously.

"Give me ten minutes. And I'll give you all the chocolate you can eat."

"You're kidding."

"Nope," she said. "Promise me you'll wait out here."

"You'd better take the car keys," I told her.

Kelly did, seizing my keys and going into the bedroom. "Don't come in until I tell you to," she said. Kelly closed the door and I reclined on the couch, waiting. I heard the water running in our bathroom.

As I waited, I got up and changed the romantic comedy DVD for a porn tape. Everything looked like candy: the pink nipples of a redhead like the opened insides of chocolate-covered cherries, her cunt like a banana split drowned in strawberry sauce. Her ass ... well, never mind about that. When she started sucking her well-tanned co-star's cock, all I could think about was *dulce de leche* ice cream bars. When he came in her dark hair, it was marshmallow sauce on chocolate.

"Come on in," shouted Kelly from the bedroom.

I killed the tape and went in.

"What the fuck?"

Kelly lay on our bed, her body naked, her pussy freshly shaved. Her back was slightly arched and her legs were spread, her arms thrust rapturously over her head. She rested on a clear plastic sheet spread across the mattress. She smiled at me, evil, wicked, her eyes sparkling and her teeth flashing from a field of glistening cocoa-coloured flesh. Her pussy, smooth, was mingled pink-and-brown. Her long legs looked like Janet Jackson's.

From the forehead down, down she was covered in

65

chocolate.

"You're crazy," I said.

"Eat me," she said.

"I fucking intend to," I told her, pulling down my sweat pants to reveal my quickly swelling cock. "If there's vanilla under all that chocolate sauce," I said, "I'm going to find it."

I didn't kiss her first – call it my one last gesture of impudence. I treated her like the chocolate-slicked delicacy she was, the living embodiment of the cocoa plant, soulless as a Snickers bar. I went right to her tits, moulding my lips to the chocolate mounds. She moaned as I lapped at her nipples, devouring the thin layer of chocolate sauce. Then I licked her face from chin to forehead, smearing and drooling chocolate

Damn her, I barely tasted the chocolate. I licked her head to toe, my tongue sliding over her belly, delving between her smooth cunt lips, lapping over her thighs. The taste was lost in the hunger of my throbbing cock. I was like the dope addict who kicks and finds he's always horny. Except William S. Burroughs never dreamed of this kind of habit.

My tongue left squiggly trails up her belly, down her arms, from knee to thigh to pussy. I turned her over, finding her backside unpainted, and put big brown handprints over her ass. Then I spread her legs and entered her, listening to Kelly moan louder as I painted obscene words on her back with chocolate-covered fingers.

When she heard me sigh in that way I do, felt me quickening the pace of my thrusts into her, she wriggled forward and pushed me onto my back. Descending atop me, she spread her thighs and settled her pussy onto my face, her mouth gulping my cock as I started to eat her

66

for real. She still tasted of chocolate, her pussy smeared with that rich, sweet taste mingled with the tang of her juices. She came almost immediately, and when I came a moment later, she lapped up my cream like it was sesame fucking tahini and she was the goddess of healthful cuisine, which she was.

Curled up against me, the plastic sheet now sticking to both of us, she licked at the smears of chocolate our tryst had left on me, my chest hair matted with globules of sauce.

"I thought you didn't like chocolate," I said. "And I *know* you don't eat sugar."

She reached out to the nightstand, picked up one of the three empty jars there, which I'd completely ignored in my fervour to devour my chocolate-covered girlfriend. She held up the jar and I took it, reading the label.

The label said: *The Naughty Chocolatier Brand Flavoured Body Paint. Also Available in Strawberry, Cotton Candy, Blue Raspberry and Passion Fruit. 100% Sugar Free.*

"You're evil," I said. "Now I'm going to have to detox from aspartame."

"One thing at a time," she said, her tongue tracing candy swirls around my nipples. "There's always tomorrow."

"I'll be fucking you with veggie burgers by the time you're through with me."

"I love it when you talk dirty," Kelly said.

The Naked Supper
by M. Christian

With legs like bags of cement, the Fat Man was led to his
regular table. Sitting in the offered chair, his creamy
mass rolled over the seat and around the straight iron
back. Nervously, he lingered over the menu, only
occasionally lifting an elephant-like head to free jowls
from stiff collar. Then, with great expertise, the Fat Man
ordered.

First, rushing out of the noise and turmoil of the
kitchens, was the bread. Buns soft as down, lying poised
and inviting on a plate. Tender to the touch, with a firm,
barely yielding, crust. Delicately parted, the buns
steamed from pale white seams – the crust delightfully
resilient, but easily kneaded and clutched by gripping
hands. The insides were velvety smooth, warm and
subtly moist. Butter streamed down tanned sides, pooling
on the plate: tempting an eager tongue. A softening cube
of brilliant yellow slipped gently by, ringed with clear,
hot fluid – bubbling around the edges and sinking into
the dough.

With a clatter, the soup was brought: a lake of liquid
ecstasy. Onions, small and nymphish, played hide-and-
seek among rafts of cheese, flirting with the spoon,

pushing up against the firm, curved shape – splashing and faintly giggling at the clumsy attempts to snare them. But for all their acrobatics and squeals of playful delight they finally surrendered, their furtive advances giving way to a ballet of fire and verve when tasted. The rest of the pool held tempting secrets, hiding them beneath a broth of warmth and stimulation.

A fragile young thing was brought to the table; so fresh and untouched. She was delicate enough to tear under brutal handling, never to be whole again, but with enough spirit to allow a hold, a grip to go onto greater things. The salmon lay sublime on a cool platter, staring out with eyes full of innocence, yet with a hidden, mischievous glimmer of wanton surrender; a quiet invitation to a ravishing. It patiently waited advances, the release of that innocence: awaiting a firm hand to take what she offered, lying there to her side. She waited for someone to consume her with mad abandon and the touch of a trained palate. The salmon eagerly awaited consummation.

A bowl was delivered: a secret forest concealing deep and mysterious pleasures. In a fold of green, hidden beneath a creased lettuce leaf, lay a subtly enticing tart. A juicy little tomato that darted through the forest and folds, from the strong support of the cauliflower to the entrancing hypnosis of the fork. Tempting disaster, the fragile thing played with the chase – filling the air with the smell of her slick, oiled skin – and then vinegar when it looked as she might be passed by.

Two breasts, upthrust and firm, golden in the sun's setting rays. Daring and obvious, challenging all comers. No innocent this chicken. Young, yes. Spring, definitely. Outrageous and provocative, stomping a shapely drumstick and demanding, in a loud aroma of heady spice, that she be consumed. Here! This minute! Now! Glistening butter rolled slowly, melting more and more with each steamy inch towards the thighs, down browned skin with the hint of hidden, pale, white meat imminent. Plucked nude, with her thighs wide apart, breasts exposed, the chicken leered and demanded – before possibly growing cold.

Pert. Good body. Excellent aroma. Full of vigour. No doubt of French extraction. Aged just enough for experience, not so young as to be easily bruised, and not too old to sour. A dazzling little '25, lazily floating in the glass, tantalizing with eager provocations. Comfortable to taste, to kiss, to embrace with lips, and to drink – just as that little tart with the good body and a distinctive heady aroma loves to consume.

A perfect cone of delight, upthrust and ready, a velvety cherry precariously poised on the brink, ready to topple into a debauchery of whipped cream and strawberry preserves. The dessert coyly avoids all advances, leaning one way, then the other. Toying, playing with and being played with. The cool dish wiggled a frosty lady-finger, inviting all comers to break her ice cream exterior and get to the rich, sweet insides.

Coffee. Steaming hot and fierce. Spicy, waiting to break free and run rampant: raising temperatures and setting hearts a-pounding with ferocity. A true Colombian spirit, bubbling secretly in a china cup, struggling to break free with steamy excitement, a mad Amazon fighting the trap.

With lips to cup, a little swish for taste – that delicate bouquet of strong urges, overriding everything else: driving the heart and raising the temperature, the blood pressure. Wild power, tickling tongues and warmed cockles. Building towards a pleasurable pain, straining for release, any release, to escape the burning, the steaming concentration – and with an exhausted sigh, to swallow the hot coffee.

Finished with his meal, the Fat Man pushed himself away from the table and leisurely smoked a cigarette.

Melting Chocolate, Crumbling Stone
by Jean Roberta

The buzzer sounded hesitant, as though the person pressing it might have chosen the wrong apartment number. Louise was not impressed. Her date, Wesley, was not supposed to be here for another fifteen minutes. A first date on Valentine's Day was guaranteed to be tricky anyway. Louise sighed. She hated starting over so soon after the last one, but she knew from experience that the best way to show an ex that she was past history was to appear in public with someone else; the lesbian gossip network would ensure that the new couple would be widely known as an Item within hours. Louise never had to stay home alone if she didn't want to.

"Louise," crackled a familiar voice, harshly distorted, "I just want to talk to you."

"I'm busy, Petra," responded the voice of an irritated babysitter. Several passers-by smirked as they walked past the humble supplicant. "It's Valentine's Day." This meant, of course: I have plans with someone who makes you look like a fool, a hayseed, a mistake of my youth.

The woman standing on the sidewalk was not ashamed. She was big, blonde, healthy and athletic, the grandchild of immigrant farmers. She was not admired for her wit, but was respected for her honesty and her physical skills. She was a connoisseur of women. These qualities had served her well in the lesbian community ever since she had first sneaked into the gay bar by lying about her age.

Petra's image had even served her well when she was courting Louise. But then, the delicious Woman (local code-word for femme) had turned on her, apparently unable to handle the amount of pleasure Petra gave her or unable to forgive her for being too rough or overwhelming, although Louise had told Petra that she had things all wrong. Two months later, the Amazon suitor was still full of remorse, confusion and other feelings that demanded an outlet.

Louise continued to prepare for her date, assuming that Petra had gone away. Looking at herself in the mirror, Louise fretted over her dark eyebrows, as usual, not realizing how much drama they added to her deep blue eyes, pale skin and cheekbones. Her long black hair was pulled into a tight braid and pinned up in a style that looked Victorian. Louise had also tried getting her hair cut close to the scalp, but nothing she did to herself could dispel her air of fragile intensity which drew would-be protectors like a magnet. The fine-boned woman had never seen the slightly sinister look that passed over her own elfin face when she was annoyed. She was ten years older and forty pounds lighter than Petra.

An urgent pounding on the apartment door demanded a response. This was downright rude, and Louise pulled the door open without making any effort to smile. Petra stood before her, somehow looking sheepish and determined at the same time, clutching a heart-shaped box of chocolates like a shy teenage boy on prom night.

"So you waited until someone opened the security

door," Louise accused. "Jesus, Petra. Do I need to get a restraining order to keep you out? Someone else is going to show up here any minute. That will be interesting. Do you want to meet her, and explain to her what you're doing here?"

Petra appeared unruffled. "I won't stay long, honey," she explained. "I just wanted to give you this – no, take it, I don't expect anything in return. Just think of it as a little divorce settlement. I also wanted to show you something else, but if you're busy, I'll just go." At that moment, the phone rang. Louise's instincts, sharpened by the pain of seeing the dyke who still moved her, told her that the call was not good news.

To Petra's delight, Louise said, "You might as well come in," then impatiently reached for the receiver.

"Uh, hello," Wesley's voice muttered. "I'm really sorry. I really am. I can't make it tonight. Something just came up, and it's too complicated to explain, but I'd really like to see you soon. Maybe we can meet for lunch later this week."

"Is there someone else at your place?" demanded Louise in the voice of a cop.

Wesley almost choked. "Well, yeah, but – I didn't invite her. She came to bring back my suede jacket. You remember Carla-my-ex, don't you?"

"Yes," snapped Louise. "I'll see you sometime, Wesley." She didn't bother to say goodbye before hanging up.

Slightly nauseous with mixed feelings, Louise turned to look again at Petra, who was seated on the sofa with hands folded, like a polite guest. Louise now noticed that Petra's short hair was decorated with clips that looked like clear plastic butterflies. The blonde was also wearing a discreet amount of makeup, silver earrings which caught the light, and a pale blue sweater which clung to her full breasts. As though Petra could not quite bring herself to wear a skirt, she was wearing expensive-looking ivory wool pants. Petra's new image might have looked convincing to Louise if she had never seen the younger dyke before. As it was, the changes looked bizarre. "You look cute, Miss Pee," smirked the hostess.

"I hope so," returned the guest with a fervour that made Louise stare. "I don't really understand it, Louise, but I hope this is what you want." The smaller woman remembered a saying: when the gods want to punish you, they give you what you've asked them for. She felt so moved that she had to restrain herself from sliding onto Petra's lap and kissing her in gratitude, in the style of their past relationship.

Groping toward a new role, Louise sat down and held her guest's hands with a pressure that she hoped would transmit both care and control. "What don't you understand, baby?" she demanded.

"You!" Petra burst out. Louise saw with approval that the bigger woman was resisting an impulse to grab her and lift her off the sofa, as before. "You're a helluva woman, and I thought you knew how I felt about you. I didn't think I was going too far." Petra searched her mind for acceptable words which could carry her meaning. "I thought you loved it when I held you. When I had you. I know you wanted me."

"Okay," the older woman responded thoughtfully, "you're partly right. I loved what you did. I loved it so much that I wanted you to be in my place. And I wanted to be in yours. I don't think you could ever understand unless I show you. The only thing I didn't love was what you wouldn't do. Anyway, I like your outfit, honey. Let's have a drink."

75

When Louise handed Petra a rum-and-coke, her favorite drink, Petra grabbed it as though she hoped to find courage in its depths. "You could open your box of chocolates," she urged her hostess, seeking approval.

Smiling at the implications, Louise slowly pulled the pink satin ribbon from the heart-shaped box, lifted the lid, selected a chocolate-covered cherry and slid it between her teeth. "Mmm," she murmured as the chocolate melted on her tongue.

Louise then seized Petra's attention by pulling her drink away as she held a caramel-filled chocolate to her coral-tinted lips. The blonde opened them, and her hostess pushed the morsel far enough into the warm cave of Petra's mouth to give her the taste of fingers as well. Before Petra could suck them deeply, they were withdrawn. "I wonder if stone hearts can melt too," Louise mused, as if to herself. Petra turned red.

As the pet savored the sweet offering in her mouth, Louise bent down, raised her chin with two fingers and gave her a soft, slow kiss. Louise's tongue found entry as Petra felt her bones turning to Jell-o.

Cupping one of the Amazon's melon-shaped breasts, Louise grasped something unexpected: seams, wire, possibly even lace. As soon as Petra had caught her breath, she explained. "Lawn-jer-ay," she bragged girlishly. "Do you want to see?"

Louise laughed aloud. "I want you to dance for me, honey," she advised her guest. "See if you can seduce me by taking your clothes off to music." The smaller woman turned gracefully to pick out a disk, a chart-climbing song named "Besame, Rosita" (Kiss Me, Rosebud) sung by a caped performer known as Zorro, which was often heard from car radios in rush-hour traffic. The popular sound of guitars, drums and castanets suddenly filled the room as Louise sat back to watch and Petra stood up uncertainly, wanting to accept and surpass this dare.

Petra began to gyrate to the beat as she had seen sequinned dancers do on TV. She had a good sense of rhythm and a body which could move in surprisingly sensual ways once she had convinced herself that she was not handling a basketball. In her pastel outfit, she looked like a schoolgirl driven to distraction by her own rising womanhood and the music of her forbidden classmates, the ones her parents wanted to keep her away from. Luckily for Petra's concentration, the meaning of the Spanish words (Rosita, I'm dying, and only your kiss can save me) was unknown to her.

Gaining confidence, the blonde flirt lifted the lower edge of her sweater, inching it up over her rose-colored lace bra. As though throwing a ball toward a target, she swept the sweater over her head and tossed it to Louise, who pressed it to her nose.

Despite its wire structure, the bra could barely control Petra's bouncing breasts. In contrast, the midriff below them was taut and muscular. It attracted the viewer's attention as Petra's purposeful hands reached down to unbuckle, unzip, and ease her pants down past her hips.

After her pants had been thrown onto a lampshade, Petra turned her back to her audience and boldly shook her large, firm, rose-panty-covered ass in Louise's face. The blonde had discovered how to shimmy by moving her knees, and she sent ripples up through her flesh to her collarbone.

Louise licked her lips as Petra gracefully unhooked the front closing of her bra. Two pushy breasts burst out of captivity, revealing two hard nipples which almost matched the fabric that had confined them. Dressed only in panties, the dancer took her time sliding them down, revealing a smooth navel and an expanse of porcelain-pink skin. During a climax in the song, Petra bent to pull her panties down to her knees, then stood solidly on one foot to lift the other leg free. She repeated the process, then offered her panties, damp crotch forward, to Louise as though they were a bouquet.

Dancing naked in Louise's apartment, Petra looked like a mythical woman: a Valkyrie bathing in a stream, or a Scandinavian goddess in uncovered glory. Writhing on the floor, the big blonde spread her legs, showing wet pink lips between borders of light-brown curly hair. Her warm, slightly yeasty smell wafted to Louise's nose, mixed with the musk of sweat from hair and armpits. Too soon, the song ended.

"Don't get up," commanded the viewer, trying not to grin. "On your hands and knees, back straight. That's it." Even in this position, Petra's body radiated power. Like a champion racehorse ridden by a skilled jockey, however, she showed a particular grace when doing as she was told.

Louise was so excited that she was glad Petra couldn't see her flushed face. Kneeling behind her suitor, the smaller woman slid a firm hand down between two pink cheeks to find a puckered anus, a hairy slit, and a swollen nub of flesh which jumped when touched. "You bad girl," snickered the explorer. "Such a tease and a showoff. Do you know what you're going to get?" Louise regretfully withdrew her right hand from Petra's soft wetness to slap each bum-cheek loudly, holding a big hip in place with the other hand. Petra moaned as though she could no longer control her reactions.

Reaching down and in to tickle sensitive folds and spread wetness across slickness, Louise also tormented her pet with words. "How many of your friends know you love this, honey?" she asked with concern. "Don't you think we should tell them? Oh, that's a good spot. An itch that needs to be scratched."

Louise worked three fingers into Petra's welcoming cunt and began pumping to a calm, slow rhythm. While her fingers were deeply enveloped by eager flesh, they traced experimental designs on it, searching for magic spots which could explode what was left of Petra's self-control. "Are you close, baby?" the hostess suggested.

"Oh yeah," panted the Amazon, pushing back with force. Louise thought the female animal beneath her resembled a mare in heat: her need, like everything else about her, seemed larger than life.

Smirking like an imp, Louise gently withdrew her fingers from their warm, wet home. "Teasing slut," she scolded. "Finish it yourself." Red-faced and breathless, Petra sat up on the carpet, looking at Louise in disbelief. "Spread your legs, honey," the older woman urged. "I want to see how you do it when you're alone."

Petra was aghast. Secretly, she was hugely relieved. She had grown dependent on her own strong fingers over the past two months, never dreaming that the woman she thought she had lost would ever want to watch her solitary performance.

Petra obliged, shamelessly reaching into her own heat. She fucked herself, steadily, rubbing her touchy clit as hard as she could stand but deliberately resisting her own impulse to speed up, sensing that Louise wanted her to maintain the maddening rhythm she had started. In a minute, Petra's breathing grew even faster and louder. At the moment when her pleasure erupted, the big blonde squeezed her thighs together, trapping her own hand in a muscular vise. Louise threw her arms around the performer, kissing a scream out of her.

The resilient Amazon quickly recovered her physical composure, although the experience had changed her in some permanent way. "Is that what you wanted, Louise?" she asked, almost whispering, relaxing in the arms of the smaller woman.

"Some of it," soothed the hostess, struggling to hold her pet with the strength she deserved. "You did well, kid." Louise let her hands stroke the wealth of warm skin which pressed trustingly against her modest black cotton pants and silk blouse, chosen for a date with Wesley. Louise couldn't ignore her soaked panties or the distinct aroma of her own hunger, rising to her nose, but the novelty of her new role was so compelling that she decided not to shed it or her clothes for awhile yet. Added to the pleasure of control, the sweet ache had a charm of its own.

"I still need to taste your juice," remarked the older woman, "and I haven't gone here yet." Louise reached under Petra to push one finger into her anus up to her first knuckle. After one violent squeeze, the blonde relaxed as though she were melting.

"Anything you want," promised Petra, subtly vibrating with the fervor she brought to almost every physical activity. "But Louise?" the younger dyke asked, almost shyly. "Please don't tell everyone we know."

"Ah," sympathized the smaller woman, rocking her pet slightly. "Did you?" Louise could actually smell the embarrassment in Petra's cooling sweat. "Well, never mind," she answered her own question. "Have a chocolate, sweet thing." The small hand that approached Petra's mouth with a smearing brown square was seized and kissed. "You okay, girl?" Louise asked her silent partner.

"Um. I will be," slurred Petra, swallowing hard.

"'Specially if I can still please you, honey. The way you used to want me."

Louise pulled her lover's strong arms around her. "Oh yes," she sighed. "More than before. I don't want to give that up." Petra felt redeemed as she dared to look inward for visions of her future with the complex, uncanny little dyke who was now letting herself be held. The naked woman had a gift for living in the present, and she was not willing to give that up either.

Doing The Dishes
by Rachel Kramer Bussel

The first time I did it, I did it for love.

The second time I did it, I did it to seduce.

The third time, I was ordered to do it.

And I loved every minute of it.

No, it's not something filthy at all. In fact, it's the opposite of filthy. I'm talking about doing dishes. I know, you're thinking, how crazy is that, but please understand. I get off on doing dishes. I cannot pass by a sink filled to the brim, or anything but empty, and just keep going. I'm lured to it by some force that draws my hands under the water, into the depths of the suds and spoons and discards. Sometimes I even do it with my eyes closed.

But, just as with people, all dishes and sinks are not created equal. While I'm a pretty equal opportunity dishwasher, only certain people's dishes can affect me in that special way.

It all started with Alan. Before him, I was never much of a housekeeper and the furthest thing from a housewife as you could get. I revelled in my slovenly ways, thinking I was exerting some backwards feminist statement by being just as messy as the guys.

But in Alan's apartment, something changed. When I saw that huge pile of dishes soaking in his sink, something stirred inside of me, and I was drawn to them, almost magically, like Alice, but instead of mushrooms, my intoxicant was dishes. They weren't really soaking, most of them; they were piled so high that some spilled over onto the counter and the stove. I could tell they'd been there for ages, and I just wanted to get started on them. I stared at them, fixated. I was ready for my first fix. But when I asked, he told me not to do them. "I couldn't have you do all those dishes, there are three weeks' worth there! Don't go to all that trouble, I'll just put them in the dishwasher."

I didn't bother to point out that if it was that easy, he'd have done it already, or that so many dishes wouldn't even come close to fitting in his dishwasher. I didn't say anything, just nodded, fingers crossed behind my back.

Now, if it were up to me, all the dishwasher companies would go out of business and start making microwaves or something. We could give everyone with a dishwasher a free microwave and be done with it. Who'd want a cold, impersonal machine to do this special job? Not me. In fact, anyone dissatisfied with the policy could come to me for a very personal dishwashing. And whoever invented the dishwasher should just be banished to some island and forced to eat only with their hands.

So even though he'd asked me to leave them, I ignored him. It wasn't easy, let me tell you, to wait two whole days for him to leave the house. I didn't want to look too eager about him leaving, but when he was finally gone, and I'd made sure to hear him head down the stairs and slammed the door, I did a little dance of glee before racing over to the now obscenely piled sink.

I first turned the hot water on, holding my hands under the heated spray. I let it wash over my fingers for a few minutes, getting them used to the heat. I don't use those icky yellow gloves either; they make my hands smell like rubber, and if I were going to do that, I might as well delegate the dishes to an evil dishwasher. No, I like my dishes "hands-on."

I then went to fetch my shoes; at my height, I wanted my heels so I could reach everything more easily. Also, something about this act just calls for heels; it looks much nicer than balancing on the tips of my toes. I felt almost like I was being filmed, and wanted to look the part. Some of the plates and utensils needed soaking, so I let the water fill up and poured the liquid green soap into the mix. I lifted one plate, relatively clean, and lightly ran the purple sponge over it.

I smiled when I noticed the days-old coffee in a mug, next to the sink; there hadn't been room or he'd been in too much of a hurry. I ran the tip of my index finger around the edge of the mug, thinking of his soft lips sipping the steaming brew, then probably slamming it down on the counter before rushing out for work. I lifted the mug to my lips and gently licked the rim, wanting to stay connected to him for just a little bit longer. I'd been making progress with the dishes, and there was only about half a sinkful left.

In another mug, I found fresh remains of hot chocolate, and smiled again. How adorable. I dipped my index finger into the sludgy remains, then slowly ran it across my tongue. I felt the first shiver pass through my cunt at the taste. I took many more dips before plunging the mug under the water, erasing all remaining traces of chocolate.

As I got to the dishes, mostly steel pots, at the bottom,

I really got into it. For these, I'd have to work. I opened the cabinet under the sink, looking for a thicker sponge. I found a heavy duty one, unopened, and ripped the plastic with my teeth. I then attacked the first pot with as much vigour as I could. I had the water on full blast and was scrubbing away, so I didn't hear the door open.

Then all of a sudden, he was in the kitchen doorway, a scowl on his face. "*What* are you doing?" he screamed.

"I know you said not to do them, but I just couldn't help it. Please, please don't be mad. Actually, well, I didn't want to tell you this, but it turns me on. I've been doing your dishes for half an hour and now I'm all covered in water and turned on. Don't you want to come over here?"

He stared at me for a good minute, taking in the way my nightie clung tightly to my chest in the many areas where water had splashed onto it. I still held the purple sponge in my hand. He came towards and me and pressed my back up against the sink. The sponge fell to the floor but I didn't care. He lifted me up so I was sitting on the edge of the wet counter. "So this, gets you turned on now, does it?" he asked as he stroked me over the wet fabric of my panties.

"Yes, it does," I said, leaning back with my arms on the side of the sink. I knew I'd get him to see dishes in a whole new way, and I was right.

The next time, dishes helped me get the girl. At least, that's what I told myself.

We'd been having a pleasant enough date, but one that looked like it was going to end with a sweet kiss on the lips and an "I'll call you soon." She was going to drive me home, but said she needed to take a shower first. Well, that was a weird sign, but short of asking to join her, I couldn't figure out how to spin that into her bed.

So while she turned on the blast of the shower spray, I rolled up my lacy long sleeves, knowing they'd still get a bit wet. I didn't mind. I let the hot water run, no gloves, to feel its heat course through my body. I plunged my hands in, soaking them, scrubbing. I thought of all the commercials I've seen as a child, talking about "dishpan hands," the dreaded disease of mothers everywhere. But I liked the way my hands felt after a good scrubbing, all wrinkly and used.

I went slowly, savoring each dish. I rinsed the bowl we'd used for the salad, removing traces of oil-covered leaves. I found the knife that could only be hers (I only use forks and spoons), and slipped it into my mouth, feeling the ribbed edge and tangy metal against my tongue. Finally I slid it out and washed it properly, wondering how it would feel inside me.

I was nearing the end when she stepped out of the shower, wrapped in a robe with a towel atop her head. I could feel her stop on her way to her room and just watch me, but I didn't turn around. With the next knife I found, I again opened my mouth and slid it in, pushing it back and forth in a fucking motion that she'd have to be completely dense to miss. She walked closer, dropping the towel to the floor. She walked right up behind me and pressed herself to me. She reached for the knife and slid it into her own mouth, then pushed my head forward and trailed it over the back of my neck. I gave a startled jump, and she pressed tighter against me. She led the knife down the ridges of my back, slowly, while I tried to stand perfectly still. As she reached closer to my ass, I couldn't help but move, and I spread my legs a little wider. She was now standing a few inches away, focused on her kitchen knife. She tapped it slightly against my ass and I moaned, and she did it again, harder. I lifted my ass into the air to give her better access, but she was past that. I felt the knife about to enter the place of my fantasy from moments before. She'd turned it around, but I could feel the heavy end of the knife slowly entering my slick pussy. I moaned and gripped the edge of the sink tightly.

She slid a finger in alongside the knife handle and I felt like I would explode. She didn't move the knife too much, just a slow back and forth, but the whole experience just pushed me over the edge. My body shook and I had to hold onto the sink ever harder as well as pressing my feet firmly to the floor.

She handed the knife to me, steadied me against the counter. "Keep washing, we're not done yet."

I took a deep breath and turned the water back on. I held "our" knife under the hot spray for a moment, ignoring the ecological implications of this act in favor of watching it splash off the silver metal. She reached around me and began fondling my nipples. "Keep washing, remember," she reminded me as she twisted my nipple tightly. I kept the water going, moving slowly, not in any hurry to have her torments end. She kept on twisting my nipples, occasionally rubbing my clit as I did my best not to drop the dishes. Then she'd grab a utensil and fuck me with it, making a never-ending cycle of dishes that I was more than happy to play my part in washing, and getting dirty.

I smiled happily. Maybe tomorrow I'd start on mopping the floor.

About a year later, my dishes fetish had gained me quite a reputation. I was frequently asked over to friends' houses after dinner parties, and they'd covertly imply they wanted me to wash their dishes or outright ask me.

But this time, I was caught off guard. I'd spent the night at a kinky party flirting shamelessly with Alex, a dyke top who'd before now seemed totally aloof and unapproachable. But even while she whipped several other girls into nicely streaked creatures, with marks they would proudly be able to show off weeks later, she kept sneaking looks at me, and I could feel their heat even across the room. I couldn't even look at anyone else, just kept crossing and uncrossing my legs and wondering if my mid-thigh length black leather skirt was too short. I drank so much soda that I started to get jittery and had to keep passing by Alex to get to the bathroom. Finally, near the end of the night, she grabbed me on my way back from the bathroom. "Are you coming home with me tonight or what, you little tease?"

I don't know what came over me, but in response, I kissed her, pushing my nerve bitten lips up against hers and rubbing the rest of me against her as well.

"I guess that's a yes. Go wait for me by the door." I gathered my things in a fog and waited at the appointed spot.

We drove silently to her place, with her hand on my thigh for most of the trip. If we didn't get there soon, I was going to have to move her hand up a bit higher to get some relief. After the longest ten minutes I could remember experiencing, we pulled into a driveway. I didn't really take in the scenery, just followed her up some stairs and into a large living room filled with a thick white carpet and plush leather couch. I moved to sit down on the coach, but she grabbed the waistband of my skirt and steered me in another direction, to the kitchen. What I saw took my breath away. It was like Alan's but much, much worse. This woman owned more dishes than I'd ever seen in one place, ever. And they were scattered all over this room, on every possible surface. It was like some surreal art exhibit, with honey and chocolate sauce and spaghetti sticking to each item. It looked like a food fight had erupted amongst the foods in her refrigerator, each one battling for the title of "able to make the most damage in a single kitchen."

"I've heard about you, missy, so I had some friends make a little treat for Miss Dishes." She reached her hand under my skirt and pressed her fist against my cunt, the hard edges of her knuckles making me even wetter. "Now, I know you're just dying to have me beat the shit out of you; I thought you were going to pass out from watching me at the club. And as much as that hot little body of yours definitely deserves it, you're going to have to make this kitchen sparkle before you get any of my treats. Do you understand? Now, I'm going upstairs to rest for a while. Don't bother me unless it's an emergency. When I get back I want this kitchen perfectly clean, okay?"

I sucked in my breath and nodded, because as she'd been talking she'd been kneading my pussy in a way that brought me oh-so-close to orgasm, but then she took that fist right with her up the stairs. I stared longingly behind me for a minute, before trying to figure out how to tackle this mess. Well, the first thing to do was strip. I threw my clothes into the only clean corner of the place I could find, and set to work.

I brought all the dishes over towards the sink and stove. Then I started with the silverware, even though conventional wisdom says that with any major project you're supposed to tackle the larger items first. But that's never worked with me. The silverware is like foreplay. I can go quickly, stacking the shiny spoons and surprisingly sharp forks, and I get to hear them jingle

89

together. I like to build up the anticipation before I get to a really huge pot, one I can linger over and fondle.

But before I got anywhere near the pots, Alex came back. She stared at me from across the room, barking orders, telling me to work faster or to go back and redo a certain plate; how she could tell the state of its cleanliness from ten feet away I don't know, but apparently she could. As soon as she'd come downstairs, I'd started getting wet (again), and was nervous that some of my juices my might dribble down my thigh in excitement. But her voice would brook no argument, and truth by told, that's why she made me wet. She started marching closer to me. I felt like we were at boot camp or something when I noticed she had a miniature alarm clock. She set it for five minutes. The sink still held an overabundance of dishes, plus the kitchen itself looked like a war zone. There was seriously no way I could get it all done.

She held a whip in her hand. "Bend over, right here," she instructed, next to yet another pile of dishes. "Since you don't seem to be doing too well the traditional way, I'm going to have you lick these plates clean. Go ahead, I want your tongue on that top one there." No sooner had my tongue reached out than she started spanking me, first with a light hand and then much more firmly. She meant business. My tongue lapped and lapped, wishing the dish was her pussy. I had to work frantically to get through even one dish. I did, somehow getting it to look relatively clean, though who she'd get to eat on a licked-clean plate I didn't know.

"Good girl, now, let's move along." She placed the clean plate in its own new pile and presented me with more. Some had chocolate sauce, but even that was hardening. She took pity on me, reaching up to a shelf and pulling down some whipped cream, then covering the entire plate with it. "Knock yourself out." I plunged my face into the cream, not caring about making a mess (what difference did that really make in this environment?), and eager for her next strokes. This time, I went at it with gusto, and the more I licked, the harder she spanked me. Then she slipped her fingers inside me, not starting with a delicate single digit but pushing three fat fingers inside me. I could barely keep up with my whipped cream but I knew I had to if I wanted to keep getting fucked. Just as I was about to come, the alarm went off. Had five minutes already passed?

"Okay, darlin', you're off the hook for now." She blew a whistle that had been hidden in her pocket and two sexy women in French maid's outfits appeared out of nowhere. I guess I'm not the only one with a cleaning fetish. Alex led me upstairs and fucked me for the rest of the night, whispering dirty words about suds and sponges and silverware in my ear the whole time.

The Bounty Of Summer
by Carol Queen

We stop at farmers' markets whenever we're on the road, especially in August when the peaches come ripe, timed with the annual meteor showers. We get enough fruit to sate any summer hunger, not just peaches but whatever is juicy and sweet, bearing it away in brown bags like we are smuggling jewels. At the bed and breakfast we get a room overlooking the Pacific – we can see the ocean from our bed and from the huge Jacuzzi in the bathroom. It's the honeymoon suite, though we are not married, just fucking like it's the only thing we will have to do for the rest of our lives. We've come equipped with candles to make the Jacuzzi room a wet cathedral of fuck. We stay in the water all weekend, except when we're in the bed. We get out to pee and refill the water bottle so we don't pass out and drown.

We float one at a time, holding each other's heads. He can reach my pussy too because his arms are so long. He sits on the tile edge while I suck his cock, then we switch places. I brace myself on the edge while he fucks me, and we fuck as often as possible. It doesn't matter if he's hard – we both have fingers and tongues, and a bag of sex toys too if it comes to that.

He tells me to close my eyes: His voice is my blindfold. His hands roam on me everywhere, warm, wet as the water. He has turned on the jets and positioned me over one. Everything about me is open, so open, except my eyes. I can picture him anyway, his hands covering my breasts, sliding down, sliding back up to grasp the back of my neck, pulling me in for a wet and melting kiss. I float in his touch, in our sex, like a lotus on a pond, anchored.

A cold something interrupts the warm. Cold and completely smooth, not icy, but a shocking cool compared to warm water and hot kisses. He runs the thing up and down my body, rolls it, really; it seems round or ovoid. I still do not open my eyes. Over my nipples, the coolness tugging them into even tighter erection. Down my belly, giving me the ripply butterfly feeling I sometimes get when I'm touched there. Between my legs, of course, everything we play with goes between my legs, smooth and chill on my clit, nuzzling my cunt lips apart.

It feels like it wants to enter me, nudging the way his cock does, and rounded like a cockhead; but so much cooler than his cock, a little bigger too perhaps. Pushing in – he's lubed it, whatever it is, it stretches the lips, slides in and in. He makes sure it happens slowly. It is big, I realize, not the size of a fist, but big enough that I have to fight with myself a little to take it.

Suddenly it slides all the way in – it's passed the midpoint and the slide is unstoppable – I'm filled.

He tells me to open my eyes.

There on the edge of the tub one of our paper bags of fruit sits open, full of gleaming red plums not quite the size of a fist.

"Do you want another one?" he asks, and holds one up

for me to bite, juice running down my chin, down my tits.

Ah, the bounty of summer. We eat more plums while he fucks me, his cock nudging the fruit and barely fitting, juice running everywhere. Laughing.

Double Espressos To Go
by Thomas S. Roche

"For here or to go?"

She looked at me pointedly, her eyes dropping down and rising up again to meet mine.

"Coffee has a strange effect on me," she whispered.

"Let's sit and drink it here," I told her. "I need to get out of the house."

I saw her blush slightly. "All right," she said.

The saucy barrista poured our espressos, pretending not to notice that both Meredith and I were glancing at her large breasts and wondering at the way that they defied gravity, braless in their tight crop-top. I took my coffee and led Meredith through the long hallway that would take us to my favorite cafe's patio. She followed with her own espresso, cradling the porcelain cup nervously.

New lovers, we had just spent Saturday and Sunday locked in my apartment fucking more times than I, for one, could count. We had a date on Friday, intending to go to a party. Halfway through our dinner conversation it became clear we weren't going to make it. I had plans to barbecue in the park with friends on Saturday afternoon, tickets for a concert Saturday night. The tickets went unused and my refrigerator was still stuffed with chicken-apple sausages and marinated tri-tip steaks, my pantry with hot dog buns and Kaiser rolls. Sunday was all about catching up on work, trying to get a head start on the week ahead. I was still behind.

Now it was Monday morning, 8:00 a.m. Meredith and I were both sleepy and haggard, not having gotten much sleep between Friday and now. The sex was incredible, so good it never seemed like a good time to stop. Every muscle in my body ached from repeated strain as our bodies pulsed together in insatiable hunger. My skin ached in starburst patterns from the back of my thighs to the small of my back, in a bruised armband around my shoulders and down my chest and belly to just above my cock, ravaged by Meredith's love bites. Her apartment was across town and we'd never quite made it there to pick her up a change of clothes. She had been forced to borrow a T-shirt from me, going without panties under her well-used Friday-night jeans. I had all but destroyed her bra ripping it off of her some time Saturday afternoon, or maybe it was Sunday. As a result, her breasts stretched my white T-shirt in the most fetching way possible, showing every contour of her ample curves and the firm peaks of her nipples, hard in June's morning chill. I could feel my cock aching every time I looked at her – trying to get hard, but too exhausted from a weekend of fucking to even seriously consider it.

I knew that under that clean white T-shirt, however, Meredith was as bruised as I was, hickies and bite marks drawn all over her luscious breasts, her smooth belly. Her thighs, too, where I'd tormented her with nibbles before feasting for hours on her cunt. My tongue hurt almost as much as my cock, and that's saying something.

We settled at a patio table under the fragrant

magnolias. The sun was out and the air was warming, but it was still chilly. Meredith's prominent nipples became more obvious under the T-shirt, drawing my eyes temptingly over them as I blew on my coffee.

"So what effect does coffee have on you?" I asked her, fully unable to look into her gorgeous face due to my obsession with her just as gorgeous breasts.

She shifted nervously and smiled.

"It makes me incredibly horny," she said. "Scarily so."

I puzzled over that. "You had coffee Saturday morning," I said.

"Right," she told me. "Why do you think you didn't make it to the picnic?"

I mused over the vivid memory of Meredith blocking my apartment door, playfully sidestepping each time I tried to get through it. Finally she'd shoved me against the wall, dropped to her knees, and planted my cock in her mouth with a hunger that would have scared me if I hadn't wanted it as bad as she did. We'd spent the next five hours fucking fervently in every position known to man or woman.

"I thought you were just horny," I said.

"Yeah," she said, raising her cup in a toast. "Here's to horniness."

"You had coffee Saturday night, too. Remember? We were getting dressed to go out."

"And did we?" she asked.

My espresso had cooled enough to sip. I drank the hot, bitter liquid while I remembered how Meredith had seized me in the stairwell of my apartment building as we headed down to the car. Again I'd protested; again she'd wood me with first her mouth on my cock, then with her jeans around her ankles, her ass pressed hard against mine with her legs awkwardly spread as I entered her from behind on the stairwell while she cried out in ecstasy, pushing herself firmly onto my cock. I was still hoping my landlord wouldn't hear about it from one of the neighbours. Even that didn't satisfy her, and by that time she'd excited me so much that I willingly left the tickets in my pocket as I took her back upstairs and bound her wrists to the headboard with a pair of thrift-store ties. I'd fucked her until the concert was long over and she had come more times than either of us could even think of counting.

"You had three cups."

"I shouldn't have," she said. "I'm like a fiend sometimes. Sorry."

"What about Sunday morning?"

Meredith took a healthy swallow of her cooling espresso. It was half gone, now. "Remember the fire escape?"

I did. We had enjoyed a few cups each of French-press, Italian-roast, and stepped out onto the fire escape to see what the weather was like so we could know what to wear as I took her home, Meredith wearing a little silky lace robe a previous guest had left, one so short that it didn't do much to hide her slim upper thighs, still covered in the marks of my teeth. It was so short, in fact, that the curve of her perfect ass just showed beneath the hem. She'd leaned against the railing and cocked her hips just so, rubbing her ass against my crotch so that my cock hardened so quickly in my pyjama bottoms that, as she lifted the back of her robe, there was only a nudge from her behind to push the stretched-out waistband of the old pyjama bottoms down over my cockhead and let her wriggle it between her pussy lips. The robe came all the way open and anyone looking out the window from across the street would have been treated to a perfect view of her perfect tits as I reached around and gripped them, pinching her nipples and digging my fingers in to her firm flesh as I pounded her until we both came right there on the fire escape. I was still thanking my lucky stars no one had called the cops.

"Oh, my," I said. "All because of the coffee?"

"Well," she said thoughtfully, swallowing, "And your magnificent cock. But the coffee definitely contributed. I don't drink it most days. If I do, I hardly get any work done. My mind keeps … wandering."

I nodded. "You'll have an interesting day at work today," I said.

She sighed miserably, looking down into the hot black liquid. "That I will."

"I need to use the restroom," I told her, then stood up and kissed her on the cheek.

I glanced back and saw her eyeing me suspiciously as I disappeared back into the cafe. She was right to be suspicious. I didn't go to the cafe restroom at all. I went to the counter, waited through the line of work-bound commuters, and ordered.

"Four double espressos," I told the sexy barrista, still eyeing her tits. "One of them to go."

She looked at me like I was crazy.

When I returned to the patio, Meredith looked at me like I was crazy, too. But her face paled slightly, then flushed as I set the four drinks down in front of her.

"I added some milk," I told her. "So you can drink them fast."

"I can't," she said. "I have to go to work. *You* have to go to work."

I glanced at my watch, took out my cell phone.

"I'm going to be in a bit late," I said into my boss's

99

voice mail. "Car trouble."

I offered Meredith the cell phone; she shook her head and turned her attention to the first of the supplemental espressos.

"I can't," she said.

"You will," I told her. "Drink up, Jitters."

She hesitated, not sure whether she could let me tempt her back into this irresponsible wonderland where people blew off friends, concerts and work to fuck until they were raw and aching. I stood up and came around behind her, bending down low and kissing the back of her neck. She moaned softly. With a glance around to make sure no one was watching, I slipped my hands under the faded white T-shirt and caressed her tits as I gently bit the back of her neck. Her soft moan rose in volume until it was anything but soft. She wriggled uncomfortably in her chair. Her nipples were so hard from the cool morning, but they hardened more as I stroked them.

"It's already happening," she said. "You're being a bastard. I can't control myself when I drink coffee."

"Then drink more," I said. "You've already had one. Why not have another? Come on, I'm sure you've got a sick day or two."

I pinched her nipples gently, making her gasp. Then I turned her head, kissed her mouth, teased her lips with my tongue. I sat down opposite her and sipped on the cooled bitter blackness of my own soul.

"Drink up," I told her. "Tropical countries everywhere need your business. And I need your cunt."

Meredith didn't look at me as she lifted her second espresso to her lips. She sipped gingerly, then took a big gulp. When she swallowed, she looked up at me shyly, her beautiful face looking guilt-stricken, naughty and fetching in the way she pursed her lips and blushed. I love pale skin because it's easier to tell when you've embarrassed a girl. But I suspected that within minutes, Meredith would be impossible to embarrass.

"So tell me what you liked about being fucked by me," I said.

"Don't even try to make conversation," she said, lifting the espresso to her lips again. "You're a bad man. You're a very, very bad man. You're evil."

"You're the one drinking espresso," I said. "Black as night."

Without a word, she gulped the last of her second espresso. Then she moved on to her third, looking guiltier than ever but starting to show the signs of arousal even more strongly than she had before."

"I think I'll take you home and fuck you on my kitchen table," I said. "It's just the right height for that. How should I do it? Should I bend you over from behind? Or perhaps spread you out on it face-up?"

"You're evil," Meredith said.

"Maybe I'll just let you decide," I told her. "I imagine you've got some great ideas."

"You're going to get me fired, you evil, vicious sexual predator," she said, her lips curving in the slightest hint of a smile as she did it.

"Take your coffee dear. It's time to go."

It was only a short walk back to my place, and we walked through the park to give her time to finish her coffee. The park was gorgeous, cool and clean in the morning air. As she walked I let my hand slip into the back of her jeans like we were a pair of lascivious rocker kids on our way to a Saliva concert. I could feel her hips moving in time with my hand, as if she were trying to coax me deeper. I stroked the small of her back gently, teasing my finger down to the very top of her cleft. I could feel her swaying in time with my movements, and when I wriggled my hand as far as it would go into her pants, I felt her push back against me, whimpering as my finger touched her pussy.

It was so wet I found myself amazed she hadn't soaked through her jeans. As it was, I suspected we had only a few minutes until they began to drip.

I took us out of the park again and back to my apartment. She grabbed me in the entryway and shoved me against the wall.

"You're a bad man," she whispered just before she kissed me, grinding her belly against my hard cock and driving her tongue forcefully into my mouth. I could feel her pert breasts against me as she reached around and grabbed my ass.

"A man does what he is," I told her.

"Fuck you," she sighed, and pulled away from me. She turned and ran up the stairs. I followed her in a cruel saunter, taking my time.

"Get your ass up here," she shouted down the stairs, "Or I'm going to fuck one of your neighbours!"

The second we were inside my apartment, she was on me. She had my shirt ripped, buttons popping everywhere. She didn't even bother with the tie. Her face disappeared behind the white poly-cotton as she ripped at my rayon slacks and pulled my hard cock out of my pants. Her lips slid down my shaft and she moaned softly as she tasted me. I realized we'd left the door open, and kicked it shut with an awkward movement.

We didn't even make it as far as the kitchen – let alone to the bed. She all but tripped me in a classic wrestling takedown, landing on top of me and moulding her musky mouth on mine, espresso laced with my cock.

She pulled open her jeans so quickly I was sure she ripped them as soundly as she'd ripped my shirt. Her slender form twisted on top of me and she settled her pussy down onto my cock, engulfing it in one smooth thrust.

"Fuck," she groaned. "Fuck. Fuck, you are a bad man. You are a very, very, very bad man ... fuck me!"

I lifted my hips to meet her, ripping the front of the white T-shirt I'd loaned her so I could taste her luscious tits while I drove my cock up into her pussy. She hammered down on top of me so hard I thought she might break me, so I flipped her over onto her back and lifted her legs high into the air. I plunged my cock into her with violent thrusts as she clawed at me, leaving fingernail scratches across my chest. With her legs now propped on my shoulders, I reached down to caress her tits, gently at first, then pinching her nipples hard as I felt her about to come. She thrashed wildly on my cock, clawing first at my flesh, then at the floor, then flailing wildly as she knocked my phone from the entryway table and reached up to claw at my face. When she grabbed my cheeks, she pushed the heel of her hand into my mouth and I bit it hard as the height of her orgasm overtook her; my thrusts quickened as I neared my own climax, and within moments I was biting her hand harder than ever as I came deep inside her. She went rigid and remained spread wide underneath me, legs thrust up high, pussy clenching rhythmically around my cock as I filled her.

I glanced at the hall clock.

"See?" I said. "There was plenty of time for sex before work."

"Bullshit," she said. She clawed out again, reaching into my pants pocket and yanking my cell phone out.

She hit redial and pushed the cell phone to her face. I

snatched the phone out of her hand as I heard it ring.

As my boss picked up, I looked down at Meredith, whose hands had found her own breasts and were pinching the nipples roughly as she looked at me with her eyes wide and her teeth bared in a terrifying snarl of bestial hunger.

Had I gone too far?

"Morning," I said. "Looks like I'll have to be out of the office all day today."

Meredith licked her lips, wriggling her pussy back and forth against my softening cock. Even in her animal fury, she succumbed to the playful urge to wink at me.

"No, no problem," I said. "But something came up. Something important. Something very, very important, and there's no way I can postpone it."

Meredith nodded fervently, rocking her hips up and down in a tempting display of insatiability.

"No way I can postpone it," I said. "No way at all."

Table For Two
by Stephen Albrow

"I'm not wearing any panties," Lucy whispered to Ted, as she sat back down at the table for two. Ted blushed, thinking that the crusty, old waiter pouring the wine might have heard his wife's earthy comment. He waited until the waiter had gone, then he asked her if he'd just heard her right.

"Dead right," she told him. "I've just taken them off, while I was in the powder room."

Lucy giggled at the thought of what she'd just said, then she ran one of her feet along the inside of Ted's thigh. He laughed, too, confused, but intrigued by Lucy's sudden display of friskiness. She was giving him that look, that special look, the one that made it clear that she wanted to share a little quality time with her husband.

"Those oysters really must have magic powers," Ted said, then he reached below the table and gave Lucy's knee a gentle stroke. Ted normally ordered when they went out and ate, but on this occasion Lucy had taken full command, insisting that they only pick food that was known to have aphrodisiacal effects. She'd ordered oysters as an entree, which they'd taken turns in pouring into one another's mouths.

For main course, Lucy had selected a juicy beefsteak, served medium rare, with potatoes and asparagus. It was Ted's favorite meal and, just like a great big hunk of meat is supposed to do, it was guaranteed to give Ted lots of the strength and stamina that he was sure to need a little later on in the evening.

Just eating the thing seemed to bring out the beast in him. As he forked succulent slivers of steak into his mouth, his sexual appetite seemed to grow out of all proportion. Several times, Lucy caught him staring at her equally succulent breasts tucked away in her brassiere. In fact, it was the constant ogling that had given her the confidence to pop into the powder room and shed her panties, just prior to dessert.

As the waiter laid the shared bowl of vanilla and chocolate ice cream in front of her, Lucy began to slowly hitch up her skirt. She continued to lift her hemline until it was just above her stocking tops, then she reached beneath the table, undid one of Ted's shoelaces and gave him a sexy wink.

Immediately, Ted looked up at the waiter, then across at his wife and then back at the waiter. He was starting to feel like a little kid that was about to be caught doing something that he shouldn't. Nonetheless, he kicked off his shoe.

"We shouldn't be doing this, Lucy," he said, reaching below the table to take off his sock.

"The tablecloth covers everything," Lucy said, then she parted her thighs just wide enough for a game of hardcore footsie.

Still uncertain about the rights and wrongs of the situation, Ted bought himself a little thinking time by making a play for the ice cream. He took his spoon and ate a mouthful of dessert, doing his best to look totally innocent in the process. But it wasn't easy for him. Even though his foot was still yet to leave the floor, already he could feel himself blushing bright red. Then, as he took the plunge and pushed his big toe along the inside of Lucy's thigh, he found a nice surprise that gave him further confidence. Lucy was wearing stockings and garters. Ted's prick began to grow long and hard, as he brushed his toes across the silky material.

"You always wear pantyhose," he said to Lucy, as his toes detected the change in texture at the point where the sheer silk of the stocking gave way to the thicker, lace stocking top.

"Nearly always," Lucy corrected him, then she leaned across the table, grabbed a spoon and fed her husband a generous dollop of the ice cream. "That's to help keep you cool," she said, sensing that Ted was getting slightly hot beneath the collar.

As Ted ate the ice cream off Lucy's spoon, he pushed his toes past the lace stocking top and touched the bare flesh that sat beyond it. Zeroing in, he then pressed his big toe directly towards the lips of Lucy's pussy. But just as his toe brushed through her muff, the waiter came back to ask if they wanted more wine.

Instinctively, Ted shaped to pull his foot away, but Lucy's hand darted under the table, keeping it firmly in place. "Just two coffees and the bill," said Lucy, smiling up at the waiter. Her nerves were ice cold that evening, even cooler than the delicious chocolate and vanilla dessert.

Ted was not quite so nonchalant. He waited until the old man had left the table and only then did he dare to press his toes up tight to Lucy's pussy. Her lips were already wet with juices. He rubbed his toes through the juices to make them sticky, then he pressed his big toe up gently against her clitoris. Lucy sensed that he was feeling nervous, so she decided to distract him with the help of the dessert.

"Now feed me," said Lucy, tossing Ted her spoon, which he used to serve her a portion of the ice cream.

As she savoured the taste, Lucy kept her mouth open, so that Ted could see the ice cream melting on her tongue. Then, when he served her another hearty spoonful, she let some of the ice cream trickle down her chin. The dribble of ice cream dripped right off her face and landed in the crack between her breasts. "Ooops," said Lucy, as Ted reached across to brush it off. He scooped the blob of ice cream from between her tits and then licked it off his fingers. As he made a big show of how good the ice cream tasted, he used his toe to tickle Lucy's clitty with a lot more certainty than he had done earlier.

In fact, maybe he tickled a little too hard, because right then Lucy let out an involuntary squeal. It was loud enough to draw glances from several fellow diners, but Lucy knew how to deal with the problem. Still ice cool, she reached for her napkin and made it look like she was coughing, then she closed her eyes and just enjoyed the sensual feelings between her thighs. After ten years together, Ted really knew which spots to hit on her body. He applied just enough pressure to her clit with his big toe to get her nicely in the mood for some fun when they got home. Not only that, but he spoon-fed her regular dollops of ice cream, too. As her clit began to tingle, Lucy decided that chocolate and vanilla ice cream and clitoral stimulation made a combination that was pretty hard to beat.

When the coffees came, Ted swallowed his in one quick gulp. He was keen to get back home to the double bed and to lose his erection inside Lucy's pussy. However, Lucy seemed to be intent on taking her time. She sipped her coffee and toyed with what remained of the ice cream, dragging it out for as long as possible. The constant below table stimulation was making her clit really start to buzz. More than that, she was getting off on looking around at the faces of the other diners. *If only they knew*, she was thinking to herself, *if only they knew where Ted's foot was right now.*

When the waiter finally came over with the bill and some complimentary mints, she even had the nerve to keep him standing there talking for several minutes. It made her so hot to know that throughout their conversation, beneath the tablecloth, her pussy was getting wetter and wetter, thanks to the attention of her husband's toes.

Ted leaned forward, growing impatient. He couldn't work out why Lucy wanted to keep on talking to the waiter. His prick was throbbing and he was desperate to use it, so he placed his hand on Lucy's knee, then ran it up her thigh till he had reached her stocking top. She looked straight at him, as he gave her flesh a tender squeeze. The look on his face told her all that she wanted to know – Ted was totally desperate to fuck her pussy.

"Anyway, thanks for a lovely evening," she said to the waiter, happy that Ted was sufficiently in the mood. She waited for him to put his shoe and his sock back on, then she grabbed his hand and gave him one of the complimentary mints.

"Let's play hide and seek," she said, then she took another mint in her hand and carried it under the table. Ted had a pretty good idea where his wife would hide the mint, since he'd just been struck by a similar idea. He would often brush his teeth with mint-flavoured toothpaste before going down on Lucy. That minty tingle was really something else!

Ted threw down three twenties to cover the bill, then he waited for Lucy to adjust her dress, ready to leave the restaurant. It was a warm, moonlit evening and, when Ted suggested a taxi, Lucy insisted that it would be much more fun to walk. She knew exactly where she wanted to take him – the doorway in the alley round the back of Kennedy's Bar, where they used to make out as teenagers.

"You remember this place, don't you?" Lucy said to him, as they came to the deserted alleyway.

"Of course," said Ted, then he paused at the entrance, as Lucy ran down to the hidden doorway. Ted looked down the alleyway and saw Lucy's arm extending from the doorway. She was holding out her black lace panties, dangling them enticingly towards him. "Come and find where I hid the mint," she shouted, then she dropped the panties to the floor.

It's time to be a teenager again, Ted thought to himself, as he wandered down towards his wife.

"What kept you?" said Lucy, who was leaning against the doorway. She had tugged up the bottom of her dress and tugged down the top, so that it was left scrunched up around her midriff. "A hundred bucks gets you everything, sailor," she whispered to Ted, as he pressed his body up close to hers.

Ted cupped Lucy's bare breasts within the span of his fingers, as he leaned in close to kiss her lips. On impact, Lucy's tongue shot forcefully inside his mouth, then she slid her hands down the back of Ted's pants. Her fingertips gave his buttocks a momentary squeeze, then, once again, her hands were on the move.

She undid his zipper and pulled down his pants. They

tumbled down around his ankles, taking his boxer shorts with them, as they fell.

Grabbing hold of Ted's bulbous crown, Lucy then detected something in the folds of his foreskin. "Looks like I win," she giggled, as she dropped to her knees and began to suck on his dick. As her tongue flicked inside the folds of his hood, Lucy could taste the mint that Ted had hidden in there.

"Boy, that tingles," Ted said to Lucy, as her saliva reacted with the sweetie, sending minty dribble all over his crown. The mint-flavoured wetness made his cockhead pulsate and quiver. A prickly sensation overwhelmed him. Sensing the heat, Lucy sucked real hard, so that the mint popped out of Ted's foreskin and into her mouth. She then used her tongue to manoeuvre the mint up and down the full-length of her husband's erection.

"That's too much," he said, as his entire prick began to throb.

"Then find my mint," said Lucy, jumping back up to her feet.

Swapping places, Ted got down on his knees and began to work his tongue in and out of Lucy's vagina. He could detect the fresh aroma of the mint in among the scent of the juices upon her pussy. It had gone in quite deep, though, so he had to use a finger to scoop the mint out of her hole. He then sucked upon the sweetie for a while, using it to flavour the whole of his mouth.

Once his lips and tongue were suitably minted, Ted focused his attentions on Lucy's clit. He gave it lots of sticky kisses, mixing in the occasional thrust of his tongue. The minty oral ministrations drove Lucy wild with passionate desire; a fact that she made blatantly clear to her husband.

"Fuck me, Ted," Lucy whispered, as the tingles in her erogenous zones left the whole of her body aglow with sexual feeling. At once, Ted jumped up to his feet and gave his wife a few strong kisses. During one of them, he manoeuvred his prickhead between the lips of Lucy's cunt. She then jumped up and wrapped her thighs around his body, allowing Ted to fuck her right up against the doorway.

There was no doubt just how turned on Lucy was by the ease with which Ted's prick was able to slide between her lips. Her crotch was dripping wet with sticky juices. Ted took full advantage of the extreme levels of lubrication by fucking Lucy hard and fast, right from the moment of penetration. He pumped his prick in and out of her pussy with the same kind of passionate force that he'd shown when just a horny teen. Groans of contentment fell from Lucy's lips. "Yes, yes, yes ..." she started screaming, her frenzied cries punctuating each forward jerk of Ted's erection.

As the speed of the fucking intensified still further, Ted pressed his fingers beneath Lucy's garters. He dug his fingertips into her thighs, then pressed them down the tops of her stockings. Lucy's breasts were undulating, in time with the thrusts of Ted's overeager prick, so he buried his head between her plump mounds, stilling the undulations. Slowly, Lucy twisted her upper body to the side, not stopping until her left nipple was pressing between Ted's lips.

A deafening roar erupted into the night, as Lucy thrilled to the feel of Ted's minty saliva on her swollen nipple. She screamed his name, as he continued to thrust his phallus in and out of her cunt. Then, all at once, her narrow tunnel began to convulse around his prick.

Lucy's orgasm was loud and long, the depth of

sensation helped along by Ted's increasing forcefulness. The orgasmic convulsions in Lucy's pussy had made her muscles grip extra tightly around his shaft. In order to fight his way through the muscular contractions, Ted had been forced to heighten the tempo still further. It meant that just as her orgasm started, Lucy's pussy began to receive the most explosive thrusts of them all.

"That's the great thing about a three-course meal," groaned Ted, as he easily managed to maintain the higher tempo, "it gives you plenty of energy, not to mention heaps of stamina."

Lucy groaned by way of agreement, the spasms in her cunt making it clear that she was totally satisfied with the way that her husband had chosen to burn off the calories he'd taken in over dinner. Every ounce of the steak and the ice cream and the oysters seemed to have been converted into blistering sexual energy. Ted was displaying the raw athleticism of a man half his age; never more so than during what proved to be the climactic thrust.

It was a thrust of pure animalistic power and, as Lucy's muscles closed in around his prick, Ted felt his crown starting to spasm. A jet of juices rocketed out of his cum-slit, giving further sustenance to Lucy's cunt.

On feeling his ejaculation, Lucy let out a scream, then kissed Ted fiercely. He kissed her back with just as much passion, then he dropped to his knees and pressed his face to her cunt. The pool of juices between her thighs smelled sweet and pure and deliciously minty. The desire to lick it was irresistible. Ted plunged his tongue into Lucy's hole.

"Haven't you eaten enough for one evening?" she asked him, as she closed her eyes and enjoyed the pleasant tingles.

"I always save plenty of room for my favorite course of the evening," Ted answered, then he hungrily devoured his wife's post-orgasmic cunt.

And Lucy knew exactly what he meant by that. The oysters had been magical, the steak totally awesome and the ice cream and the complimentary mints a real joy to the palate. But it was the final course that Ted and Lucy would remember for the longest time. Food is great, but you can't beat having the one that you love for dessert.

Breakfast In Bed
by Violet Taylor

Mia relaxed into the bed as Pierre licked his way down her neck to her breasts. The tray that held their breakfast occupied the corner of the bed, the remnants of crumpets and lemon curd mingled with the stems of cherries and a few bright-red strawberries still beckoning to her. As Pierre suckled her firm nipples, Mia sighed and relaxed into the sensations. She reached out and plucked a strawberry from the tray, bringing it to her full lips and closing her eyes so she could savour the taste of the fruit as she enjoyed the feel of Pierre's mouth on her nipples.

To her surprise, her lover reached up and snatched the strawberry from her hand.

"Uh-uh," he said. "If you want to eat, you'll have to earn it."

"Oh, I will, will I?" said Mia. "A moment ago we were both gorging ourselves.

"Times change. Breakfast is over. We're making love now." Pierre drew the moist strawberry down Mia's belly; its coldness made her skin goosebump and made Mia squirm. He licked his way after her and slipped the strawberry past her smooth pubis and pressed it against her pussy.

Mia gasped as the cool strawberry penetrated her, its stem held firmly by Pierre's expert hands. Her pussy was quite wet, not just from her own juices but from the moistness Pierre had left there when he had licked her to climax just before breakfast. As Pierre rubbed the strawberry against the entrance to Mia's cunt and slipped it in, he thumbed her clitoris gently, and Mia felt her warmth rise as she began to juice more prodigiously. The rough tip of the strawberry came out of her and teased her clit, replacing Pierre's thumb as he brought his hand to her breast and began to pinch her nipple.

"So how do I earn a strawberry?" she asked breathlessly.

"By getting it good and wet," he said, and pushed the strawberry all the way into her, making Mia bite her lip as his fingers opened her wide. Quickly, Pierre seized another strawberry, and without preamble pushed it into Mia's moist pussy. The coolness and roughness of the fruit brought an unexpected sensation to the inside of her cunt, and she could feel herself growing wetter as his fingers explored more fully, tucking the strawberries deep inside her.

"That's the rule for this morning," he said. "From now on, you can only eat what you fuck. And you must eat everything you fuck. Understand?"

"All right," moaned Mia as she saw Pierre's hand selecting a handful of whole strawberries and cherries. Mia began to moan as he teased her clit with each berry before inserting it. She arched her back as he inserted each morsel of fruit into her, his fingers pushing her open as he filled her with them. The cherries felt smooth, but their stems were prickly; the strawberries, covered with the fine texture so familiar to her other lips, abraded her slightly as he inserted them. But as her wetness

116

increased, they slid more smoothly, and her swelling pussy gripped the fruits more tightly, crushing them. The fruits were overripe and felt soft inside her, soon her pussy felt quite full, stuffed with the remains of their breakfast.

"I hope you're hungry," said Pierre, as he forced another strawberry into Mia's pussy; finding that it had nowhere to go, he pushed harder until it melded with the crushed berries deep inside her. A steady stream of thin red juice began to ooze out of her cunt, and Pierre bent low and began to lap it up.

"Can't let it stain the bed," he said, as Mia felt his warm tongue delving between her lips, suckling the sweet juice. She moaned as his tongue explored her. She was close to coming already, but she should have known Pierre would never let her come that easily. Instead, he rolled her onto her side and slid up behind her, reaching for the bottle of lube that they always kept by the bed.

"No," she breathed. "You can't ..."

"Trust me," he said. "You only have to eat what you fuck. My cock doesn't count."

Pierre rolled her onto her belly and she felt the cold drizzle of lubricant between her cheeks. He added some to the head of his cock and guided it into her ass, still open and accessible from the good fucking he had given it late last night. He guided her back onto her side and penetrated her from behind, his cock filling her ass until it pressed firmly against the channel stuffed tight with fruits. His arms coiling around her, Pierre began to fuck her.

"How do you feel?" he asked.

"Full," Mia gasped as Pierre's cock plumbed deep inside her ass.

"But you're still hungry?"

"Yes," she moaned softly.

She felt his fingers pulling open her lips, seeking one of the strawberries that remained there, crushed by the swelling pressure of her tight pussy. He eased one out and brought it to her lips; she eagerly accepted it and tasted the salty tang of her cunt juices mixed with the sweetness of the fruit. Her orgasm started as she felt his fingers prying her open again, seeking another fruit; the steady fucking in her ass brought her over the top and she clawed at the bedsheets as Pierre pushed another strawberry into her mouth. This time the taste of her cunt was stronger, and the berry was much softer, all but crushed by her pussy. When her orgasm subsided and she looked down, she could see the sweet juice of strawberries and cherries staining the bed obscenely. Pierre kept fucking her from behind as he produced another strawberry from her cunt and brought it up to Mia's lips. She eagerly ate it, her hungers having mingled together in one rush of lust. She reached down and held her pussy wide for him as he slid three fingers into her to find the next piece of fruit, and he came out with two, which she ate hungrily, tasting more and more of her cunt mixed with the sweetness. The whole time, Pierre never let up his rhythm inside Mia's tight behind, and she knew she was going to come again before he was finished. She ate each morsel he brought to her mouth with his red-stained fingers, licking his hand as she did. When he had to push as far in as he could go, with all four fingers, to find the very last cherry, which had wedged itself deep inside her, she came again. She couldn't be sure if it was the pressure on her pussy from Pierre's hand, or the steady fucking he gave her behind – it seemed likely that it was a combination. She came hard, moaning as Pierre slipped the final pussy-glazed cherry into her mouth. She took the stem in as well, using her skilled mouth to pluck the cherry from it and – even as Pierre continued fucking her ass – she managed to spit out the pit and do the trick she'd been so proud of in high school.

She reached back and brought Pierre's hand to her lips, then deftly spit out the tightly tied cherry stem.

Could it be that demonstration of oral skill that led Pierre to tug his cock out of her ass and smile down at her?

"I'm going to go wash," he said. "There's one more thing that's been fucking you. And you remember the rule, don't you?"

Mia lay there, her pussy throbbing with post-orgasmic spasms She heard the water running as Pierre washed his cock; her mouth watered as she anticipated the last succulent course of her breakfast. Strawberry juice smeared across her thighs and lower lips, dampening the trimmed thatch of her pubic hair. When Pierre returned, Mia looked up at him expectantly and eased over to the side of the bed so that her head hung off, her mouth open and her eyes closed.

Pierre was still quite hard; he guided his cock into Mia's mouth and began to pump, gently at first as she suckled him, then more firmly as her skilled tongue coaxed him toward an orgasm. When the hot stream exploded into her mouth, Mia gulped it as eagerly as she had eaten each thing that had fucked her that morning; its salty taste mixed deliciously with the sweet of the cherries and strawberries, and the tangy essence of her cunt.

Mia sucked Pierre until he'd given her every drop of come, then licked him all over, looking up past his cock and into his eyes as he watched her.

"Did you like your breakfast?" he asked.

"I don't know," she said. "I'm still hungry. Besides, we've made quite a mess."

"There's a very easy way to fix that," he smiled, and pushed her back onto the bed, spreading her legs as he descended between her thighs. Mia moaned as Pierre shared the breakfast he had given her, licking the sweet juice leaking out of her pussy, glazing her thighs, matting her pubic hair.

"Breakfast in bed," Pierre said as he came up to kiss her with his red-stained, sweet-tangy-salty lips. "I think this is a new Sunday tradition."

"No pancakes, though," Mia said.

"We'll find a way," smiled Pierre wickedly, and reached out to grab a scone.

Forbidden Fruit
by Ric Amadeus

At noon, she entered his study with a plate of food. He had been up since five, disturbing her only slightly as he climbed out of bed. She had spent the morning picking fruits from their organic garden, while he worked tirelessly to complete his research paper.

"Lunch, darling?"

"I'm too busy," he said, fervently working his scientific calculator as he scribbled and erased, scribbled and erased on a tattered sheet of quadrille graph paper. A half-dozen books were spread across his desk: Pesticide Residue in California Watersheds, Malathion Studies Annual, Ethnobotany Digest 1984, Problems in Biochemistry, Agricultural Pest Control and Cancer, Bug Spray and You. His computer flashed long strings of numbers, the pop-up window showing a blue bar slowly creeping past 24% as it worked on calculations needed to prove his thesis.

She set the tray down on top of his papers and leaned against the edge of his desk, well aware that her pink bikini top, a fetching and saucy garment with cherries adorning the pink fabric, didn't hide much of the fetching swell of her breasts. Her tight jean shorts were unbuttoned at the top, revealing the matching cherry-print bottoms underneath and the candy-red tattoo of an apple just above the waistline of the low-cut bottoms that featured the scripted legend: ORGANICALLY GROWN. Her long, smooth legs were dusted with the soil of the garden, and her smooth belly swelled slightly from all the organic morsels she'd eaten as she picked. The tiny bulge accented the sparkling silver ring through her navel and the tattoo. Her full, kissable lips were still stained red with the juice of organic cherries.

She said, "Baby, you've got to eat."

He looked up at her angrily, pushed his chair back, and sighed.

"But I'm close to solving this problem," he said. "I'm close to establishing beyond the shadow of the doubt that pesticide consumption is responsible for the destructive and uncontrollable rise in chronic hypersexuality in adolescent females."

"Adults, too?" she asked nervously.

"That remains to be seen," he said, his eyes narrowed and his lips pursed. "Further study is needed."

"But you should eat," she said. "You didn't even have breakfast."

"I had a cup of coffee," he said defensively. "The organic decaf Guatemalan."

"We're out of soy milk," she said.

"I drank it black," he told her.

"If you lose your strength, you'll never prove your thesis." She bent down low and kissed him on the cheek, her barely-clad breasts gently brushing his arm. "Take a break, have some food, and you'll feel so much better. Everything will become clear after lunch."

He sighed, took off his glasses, rubbed his eyes. "All right," he said. "I'll have some lunch."

"Come sit on the couch with me," she said. "It's good to get away from your desk." She picked up the tray and carried it over to the small, tattered sofa that adorned his study. She set the tray on the coffee table while he joined her, looking grumpy and angry that she was making him eat. This sort of thing happened frequently, though; he was such a dedicated scientist that he very often forgot to nourish himself – ironic beyond measure for a man whose lifework lay in proving the dangers of pesticide use and the advantages of organic farming.

She knew that once he ate, everything would seem different.

She poured him a glass of thrice-filtered water and took the unbleached cotton napkin off of the beautiful assortment of sliced apples, cherries, oranges, unyeasted home-baked bread and yogurt-cultured soy cheese that she had prepared for him.

"I guess I am pretty hungry," he said, and seized a piece of bread. He ate quickly, piling three slices of soy cheese on three slices of bread and adding a small slice of apple to each.

"The one thing I can't figure out," he said, holding a fragrant morsel near his lips, "Is what kind of affect this pesticide-induced hypersexuality would have on a man. The data is clear for young women – with improper pesticide use, they become completely unable to control themselves."

"Explains a lot," she said, leaning back into the softness of the sofa and propping her shapely legs on the coffee table. "You know, I'm younger than you."

He waved his hand dismissively. "But you've been raised on organic produce. Thank God for your parents, particularly your father. If it hadn't been for his critical early work in nourishing you entirely on organics, I

123

might never have been able to carry the torch. Now, I'm close to a breakthrough."

Her eyes lowered and she flushed slightly. She looked at the food poised so teasingly near his mouth.

"Eat your apple, darling," she said.

He stuffed his mouth full of food and washed it down with filtered water, barely taking time to chew. As he swallowed, his eyes narrowed.

"Is that your new swimsuit you're wearing?" he asked.

She smiled shyly, running her hands down over the full swells of her ample breasts. The nipples had begun to peek through the pale fabric.

"Yes it is," she said. "But I don't think I could get much swimming done while wearing it."

"That's for sure," he said.

"Do you like it?"

His eyes widened and he drank in the beauty of her tits while he chewed another slice of apple. "I love it," he said. "Fuck, it's amazing. Your tits ... your tits are incredible."

She smiled. "You never call them that."

"I guess I don't," he said, his mouth stuffed so full she could barely understand his words. "God, they're magnificent. Why have I never noticed how magnificent they are?"

"I remember you thinking they were magnificent last night," she said, smiling.

"Did we make love last night?" he mused, reaching for another apple slice. "I can't recall. My mind must have been engaged."

She frowned bitterly.

"Have another slice of apple, dear. They're good for you."

As he chewed, his eyes grew wider and he seemed unable to take them off of her tits. She could see his cock swelling in his polyester pants, stretching them noticeably. She looked at him and licked her lips.

"Would you like to see them bare?" she asked.

"I need to get back to work," he said, his voice hoarse. "As soon as I'm finished eating …"

"No harm in looking while you eat, is there?" she asked, and pulled the front of her bikini top down.

His eyes, now as wide as they could get, drank in the lush beauty of her full tits with their pink nipples. He absently placed another apple slice in his mouth and chewed as she ran her fingers over her breasts, pinching her nipples gently.

"Nice, aren't they?"

"Beautiful," he uttered in a barely comprehensible mumble around half-chewed pieces of fruit. His hand had found its way into his crotch.

"Do you realize you're stroking your crotch, darling?" she asked.

He swallowed. "Am I?" he muttered absently, rubbing his cock more firmly through his pants. "God, I can't take my eyes off of you."

"You don't need to," she said. "Keep eating." She reached out and handed him another three slices of apple, then unfastened her bikini top and slipped it off. She tossed it away so that it draped over the plate of food. She began to caress her own tits.

"You want to touch them, don't you?" she asked. "They're like ripe fruit to you. Ripe … organic … fruit."

"I can't," he said, stroking his cock with one hand while he stuffed food into his mouth with the other. "I need to work."

"What's the harm in a little touch?" she said. "But

wait, there's more of me to touch. She pulled down her shorts and wriggled out of them, planting one foot up on the back of the sofa so that her calf brushed his shoulder. The cherry-print bikini bottoms were so skimpy that he could see the swollen lips of her pussy around the crotch, poking out from where they'd been tugged free as she bent over in the garden.

"Oh my God," he burbled through apple and soy cheese. "That's so magnificent." His fingers tightened around the swell of his cock, and as she lifted her legs high in the air and peeled off the bikini bottoms, he moaned softly through fruit pulp and began to stroke faster.

"Fuck," he moaned as she spread her legs wide, lifting her hips so he could better see her ripe, open pussy with its glistening sheen of sexual juice. "That's incredible.

She reached out, wriggled her fingers under the bikini top that now partially hid the plate of food, and produced an apple slice. She slid it slowly up the inside of her thighs and tucked it between her pussy lips.

"Keep eating," she told him breathlessly. "You need food."

He lunged forward desperately, knocking over his thrice-filtered water and spraying it across the floor. His mouth moulded to her cunt and he sucked down the apple hungrily, but her thighs closed around his face and she held his hair firmly, grinding her sex against his seeking mouth as he began to tongue her eagerly. She writhed on the sofa as his mouth worked her clit, and he no longer seemed interested in protesting that he had work to do. On the contrary, when finally she arched her back and moaned in orgasm, she had to pull his head away from her sex because she just couldn't take any more.

She writhed under him, her naked skin flushed, her

lips still red with cherry. She looked up into his eyes, her hunger obvious.

"Fuck me," she moaned.

As he leapt on her and fervently clawed at the fly of his polyester pants, she plucked an apple and put it in her mouth. She then seized his hair and pulled his mouth to hers, pushing the apple onto his tongue as they kissed. His cock came free and he entered her smoothly, finding her pussy wetter than his absent mind had ever noticed it to be. He moaned as he plunged into her and started fucking her with unprecedented ardour, his hands moulding to her tits as her tongue savaged his mouth between chewing motions. She cupped his cheeks with her hands and pulled his cock deeper into her, lifting her hips to meet each powerful thrust. When she came again, she wriggled close to him and begged him to take her upstairs before he finished with her.

His eyes glazed, he pulled out of her and felt her mouth on his slick cock as she licked him clean, eagerly letting her tongue caress his balls, his shaft, and his swollen head. When he bleated softly, once, "work …" she reached out and grabbed another slice of apple, stuffing it in his mouth to silence him.

When he was right on the edge of coming in her mouth, her lips left his cock and she looked up at him.

"Take me to bed," she begged.

He chased her up the stairs, shedding his clothes as he went. When she climbed abed on hands and knees and put her ass in the air, legs spread, pussy exposed and still moist from his spit and the juice coaxed forth by his hard fucking, he didn't even think to pause. He joined her on the bed and drove into her with a hunger that made her whimper in rapturous pleasure. He reached under her to hold her magnificent tits as he ravished her from behind, fucking her so hard that she came twice more as she rubbed her clit, then begged for his come inside her. He let himself go deep in her pussy and collapsed on top of her.

Within moments he was snoring, and over the next six hours he woke up only twice, when she could resist temptation no more and found her sliding her mouth onto his cock and her pussy onto his hungry mouth. Each time he satisfied her, fucking her in as many positions as either of them could come up with before finally coming inside her. His life's work was forgotten, a tangle of scattered and meaningless papers much, much less important than his insatiable hungers and her delicious, naked body.

When finally he awakened on his own, late in the evening, he did so with a gasp and a long, low moan of horror.

"What's the matter, darling?" she asked in a whisper, her face tucked against his bare chest.

"What have you done?" he sighed. "Oh, darling, what have you done?"

She cleared her throat and said nonchalantly, "Why, whatever do you mean, baby?"

"That apple," he said. "It was from the control group."

She reddened, clutched him close.

"I'm sorry, baby. You were so caught up in your work. I ... I couldn't take it any more. I needed a little attention."

"Oh, what have you done?"

She sat up and put one finger across her lover's lips. "Shhh, baby," she cooed. "At least we've proved your premise. And it works on men, too."

She cradled him in her hand, gently stroking his shaft.

It began to grow quickly hard, and she kissed her way down his chest as he moaned softly with pleasure. When her mouth found his cock, his hands came to rest gently in her long, dark hair, stroking her as her head bobbed up and down on him.

"Oh, what have you done," he moaned, but this time he sounded less convinced. "Eve, eve, what have you done?"

There was a distant hissing from the organic garden.

Spicy Saturday
by Zoe Bishop

Tony likes spicy food. He also likes to eat pussy.

Correction. *Loves* spicy food.

And absolutely, completely fucking *loves* with all his heart to eat my pussy.

Tony's the only guy I've ever been with who's as horny as I am. He's also the only guy who's ever eaten my pussy as often as I want – whenever, wherever, for as long as I want, until I come twice, thrice, four times, five times, until I beg him to stop and he still makes me come again. God, he's the best I've ever had – with just about no competition. I just have to watch Tony lick his lips and my knees go weak.

See, it's not just that he does it a lot – he's good at it. He does me so good I never fail to come, and he never stops until I tell him I'm finished. He never says no and he always says yes, and he usually says "Please, baby, please let me" even when I tell him I'm too tired or not horny or I don't need it. He begs, and I always say yes. And I always end up glad I did.

The first time we slept together, after we had sex, he went to go down on me and I told him he didn't have to. He just laughed softly and then ate me for two hours. I've never come so many times on a first date.

He's got a tongue that takes me right to heaven. He'll do it anywhere – believe it or not, after we got together I stopped wearing underwear, because I had to make it as easy as possible for him. If knew if I didn't go without, my underwear drawer was going to be empty sooner or later, anyway, because I kept losing it. In the bathroom at a friend's house, behind a bush at the park, the back room of our favorite cafe. My panties are scattered all over town; I have no real idea where. I only hope some lucky pervert's enjoying them to this day.

Underwear's overrated, anyway – and Tony could never be overrated.

He also likes spicy food – we're talking the kind of spicy that lumberjacks have competitions about. You know the kind I mean – they take big spicy chillies and eat them whole. Big bearded Yukon types reduced to tears, sobbing like little girls. Tony licking his lips and saying "More, please," and spicy, this time. Whatever he eats, he likes it so hot it would make me cry, too. He loves it hot, hot, hot. Once I tasted his food. I'll never taste it again. Sometimes I kiss him after we eat. I always have a pitcher of ice water ready when I do.

Spicy food and my pussy: Tony's only two passions in life. The two reasons he gets up in the morning.

You hear me complaining? Not a peep. More like a moan. Even when he decided to combine the two.

He'd been cooking all day, preparing his favorite spicy dish – chilli with fresh peppers. We were having friends over for dinner, and they'd be here in about an hour. I stopped in to the kitchen to check and see if Tony needed anything.

"Anything I can do?" I asked. "You need any help?"

Tony turned, took me in his arms, and kissed me. I just about melted against him. It was Saturday; I was wearing a little sundress and nothing underneath. The house was hot from all that cooking, and it was a warm day outside. Tony pushed me back toward the kitchen table.

"Yes," he said, snatching a small green pepper from the pile next to the simmering pot. "I need to know if this pepper is spicy enough."

He kissed me again, forcing me back. I would have protested, but my mouth was full of his tongue.

I felt the edge of the table against my ass, and Tony pushed me up onto it. He dropped to his knees and I saw there was a paring knife in his hand just as he started to nudge my legs open.

"Honey," I asked him nervously. "What are you doing with that knife?"

He nudged my legs open all the way and said "Trust me."

He held up the pepper and with the deftness that came from a lifetime as the world's best amateur cook, he made six quick slits down the outside of the pepper. He tossed the knife onto the counter, looked up at me, and winked.

"Honey," I said. "I hope you're not going to …"

"Serrano chillies," he said. "Very spicy. But do you think it's spicy enough for me?"

I watched wide-eyed as the little green pepper disappeared into my pussy. It took a moment to hit me, as the pressure milked the spicy juice out of the pepper. When it did, I shrieked.

"Oh God," I gasped. "It's hot!"

The burning sizzled my cunt, the intense sensation making my clit stand immediately at attention. Tony

132

slipped the pepper out, but that only let a little hint of air in – which made my pussy burn more. My pussy swelled and tightened, my lips puffing out even as the opening tingled and ached. My clit began to throb. Tony swept the pepper up and squeezed it over my clit, and I felt the cool dribble of the pepper juice on it – cold, freezing cold, until the heat struck. Then, my clit was on fire.

"Oh, fuck you," I moaned. Ow, ow, ow, ohhhhhh …" The pain mixed with a curious kind of throbbing pleasure as my clit got so hard I thought I was going to come right away. Tony squeezed the pepper some more and another few drops covered my clit. The pain was intense, but so was the pleasure. I could feel the heat of his mouth close to my cunt.

"Oh God," I said. "You are evil."

"I'm sorry," he said. "Let me kiss and make it better." Taking the pepper away, he buried his tongue between my lips, hungrily devouring the spicy juice even as my pussy and clit heated painfully. I moaned and leaned back onto the table, lifting my hips as he put his hands under my ass and pressed me to him like a chalice. His tongue started doing what he's best at – making his girlfriend moan. The sizzling, tingling sensations mounted, and my clit felt so sensitive that I was afraid he might have actually burned it.

But then it seemed to swell still more, pulsing with blood, and Tony's tongue made me bite my finger, hard, to keep from screaming.

"Don't stop," I moaned, and came, my whole body consumed by the fire in my clit. He kept licking eagerly as I rode him, my hips pumping with the mingling of heat and succulent warmth. He drank the pepper juice from my pussy and when he was finished there was still a lingering heat, the painful swelling of my clit, which I knew would be there all night, reminding me of him as we visited with our friends, as they commented on how spicy the chilli was.

"You bastard," I whispered. "I've never come that hard."

"What do you think?" he asked. "Spicy enough?"

I eased myself off the table and put my arms around my boyfriend as he stood up. I let my hands slide down the front of his loose jeans, into his underwear, squeezing his hard cock. I shifted back and forth uncomfortably, my cunt and clit throbbing with intense heat. It made me want him again – want to fuck.

I put my lips to his ear and began to undo his pants.

"I'll show you how spicy it is," I said as I took his cock out and climbed back onto the table.

Thanksgiving Dinner
by Elizabeth Colvin

When the cab pulled up to the house, Aaron cursed softly. It was dark. Serena's family tended to go to bed early, but he'd held out hope that he wouldn't have missed everything. Not because he had such a passionate need to share Thanksgiving with Serena's family, but because he felt guilty about having missed it. Not that he could have changed anything.

As he hauled his suitcases up to the front door, wondering how he was going to get in without waking everyone, the front door opened and there stood Serena, wearing nothing but a long T-shirt that hung to mid-thigh. Well, not really mid-thigh – more like barely-thigh, decent by one or two inches. Aaron hadn't seen her in a week, and his eyes roved appreciatively over his wife's lithe form. She smiled at him.

"The prodigal husband," she said, opening the screen door and kisses him. "Everyone's gone to bed except me."

"Shit," he said. "I knew that would happen. Well, flying on Thanksgiving, what did I expect?"

Serena pulled him into the warm house and closed the door, then pressed him against the wall, kissing him. He set down his suitcases and embraced her properly, feeling his skin tingle as her nipples hardened through the thin cotton shirt against his chest. He could feel his cock starting to stir in his pants, and as Serena leaned against him she noticed it, too. Her hand brushed against the front of his pants, squeezing his cock lightly. She smiled.

"Hungry?" she asked.

His eyes flickered up and down her body, particularly lingering on the way her erect nipples distended the shirt, before he answered.

"Famished," he said.

"Good. I managed to save some food for you. We're staying in my old room. Why don't you change into something more comfortable and I'll get a plate ready?"

"All right," said Aaron, his hand slipping down to his wife's ass and giving it a playful squeeze.

She slapped his hand away. "Don't get cocky," she smiled. "I know it wasn't your fault, but you've still got to make it up to me. Being so late, I mean."

"Any way you want," he said. "Your wish is my command."

"You have no idea what you've just said," smirked Serena as she walked into the kitchen, the shirt riding up just far enough to show Aaron that she was wearing his favorite pink panties.

Aaron mounted the stairs, his stomach grumbling and his cock starting to get hard.

When Aaron came back downstairs, he'd changed into sweat pants and a T-shirt. The living room was lit dimly by a single lamp on the end table. Serena was curled up on the couch, her feet tucked under her ass, her own T-shirt up high enough to show the panties underneath. The silky fabric glinted in the slanted light. A plate sat on the coffee table, covered with a single white napkin.

He reached for the napkin. "What's for dinner?"

Serena caught his wrist neatly. "Uh-uh," she said. "I said you had to make it up to me, and I meant it. This is how."

Smiling, she held up a leather blindfold.

"You've got to be kidding me."

Serena shrugged, playfully tossing her hair. "If you don't care enough to show up to Thanksgiving dinner on time, you certainly don't care about what you get to eat, now do you?"

"But the flight …"

"Oh, I know all about that," said Serena. "Don't make excuses. Put on the blindfold or go to bed hungry." She tossed her hair again, more flirtatiously this time, and her full lips curved upward in a smile. Her eyes flickered up and down Aaron's body, lingering briefly over the half-hard cock that bulged in his sweat pants.

"In more ways than one," she said.

Aaron thought for a moment. "Your parents are really asleep?"

"Like rocks," she said. "Besides, after the Fourth of July experience they know better than to come into the living room when we're up."

"All right," said Aaron, taking the blindfold and putting it on. He settled into the soft couch as Serena grabbed the plate and settled onto him, her knees bent over his lap as she leaned against the arm of the sofa.

"Hands down," she said. "Just pretend it's a lap dance."

"Lap dances aren't done blindfolded."

"This one is," she said. "Hands at your sides."

Aaron obeyed, tucking his hands under his thighs. He felt his arm brushing Serena's thigh, and its smoothness brought goosebumps to the skin of his arm.

137

"Open your mouth," she said.

Aaron obeyed, feeling a little nervous about what he was going to get. He felt Serena shifting slightly, and then felt her fingers slipping into his mouth. He accepted a morsel of turkey, chewing quickly, his stomach rumbling.

"Slowly," she said. "Savour it."

"I'm starving," he said.

"If you'd rather go to bed hungry …" Serena wriggled her body, rubbing her thighs against Aaron's growing cock. He slowed his chewing, savouring the juicy taste of the cold turkey.

"Like it?" she asked, perhaps unconsciously leaning the back of her knee against Aaron's crotch.

"Enough that I wish my hands were free," he said.

"Too bad. Open."

Serena's fingers entered his mouth again, this time bearing a warm chunk of microwaved stuffing. Aaron licked her fingers clean, the familiar feel of her fingers in his mouth coaxing his cock into full erection. The rich taste of the stuffing made his stomach hurt for more. When he swallowed and opened his mouth again, her fingers entered bearing a green bean, then a candied yam, then more stuffing and another piece of turkey. Each time he licked her fingers clean; each time she had to remind him to chew slowly and savour it. The taste of the familiar food, which he was expecting around three in the afternoon and had been anticipating since long before that, sent a warm, comforting glow through Aaron's body. More, though, the touch of Serena's thigh on his cock is what made him glow, and what made his cock pulse with each slide of her fingers deep into her mouth.

"All right," she said. "This is getting messy. Sorry, dear, but your skills as a moist towelette leave something to be desired. I'm going to go get a towel. Would you like some wine?"

"Yes, please," he said.

"Red or white?"

"Surprise me," he answered.

"Of course," she said, and kissed him once on his greasy lips before climbing off of him. "Don't touch a thing while I'm gone."

He sat there obediently with his hands under his thighs, but he couldn't decide if he was more tempted to reach out and grab the plate of food or reach down and grab his cock. He found himself surprisingly aroused by the touch of Serena's body against his, of her smell mingling with the aroma of the food. When she returned and sat in his lap again, he could have sworn she was going out of her way to rub her ass against his cock.

"Wine coming," she warned him. She placed the rim of the glass to his mouth and slowly tipped it; he managed to swallow two mouthfuls of the rich red wine before he dribbled some on his T-shirt.

"Uh-oh," said Serena. "Time for that to come off."

Before her could stop her she'd pulled his shirt up to his chest, and was bending down, licking and suckling his nipples. His cock gave a surge as her teeth closed gently over one nipple and her tongue flicked it. When she lifted the shirt higher, he obediently put his arms up and let her take it off of him.

She embraced him and Aaron felt the naked curve of her breasts against him. She had taken her shirt off. Her nipples, very hard now, rubbed against his chest invitingly.

He had to fight to keep sitting on his hands.

When she told him to open again, he received a succulent morsel of candied yam, followed by turkey, wine, green bean, wine, stuffing, and then a bite of a buttered roll. She wiped his face with the towel between courses, but still expected him to lick her fingers clean. When he'd finished with the roll, she bent forward and kissed him on the lips, the salty taste of her kiss mingling with the aftertaste of Thanksgiving dinner and the red wine.

"Still hungry?" she asked him, her voice breathy, when their lips parted.

"In only one way," he said.

"That's what I thought," she said, and slipped off of him, stretching out lengthwise on the couch. "Time to make it up to me for real."

It took him a moment to get what she meant, but when she slipped her hand into his hair and pulled him down between her legs, he got the picture. She pressed his face to her pussy, and when he tasted it, naked and tangy against his tongue, he realized that she'd stripped off more than just her shirt when she'd gone to get the wine. Hungry for her, Aaron began to eat her pussy, his tongue slipping between her swollen lips to taste her wet entrance before licking up to her clit and pressing firmly and rhythmically against it. Serena began to moan.

"Right there," she breathed. "Eat your thanksgiving dinner, naughty boy."

Aaron slipped his hands under Serena's ass, no longer worried about the no-hands rule. He lifted her so he could better eat her pussy, tonguing her from cunt to clit and back again. When he focused on her clit, she reached down and grasped his hair firmly, telling him that that's where he should remain. He started licking her in the perfect rhythm he was so used to – the one that made her come. As long moments passed, Serena's legs closed more tightly around Aaron's face and her hands reached around to grasp his shoulders.

"I'm close," she breathed. "Fuck me."

Without taking the blindfold off, Aaron climbed on top of Serena and slid easily between her legs. She was so wet that his cock went in easily, smoothly in one thrust. She bit his shoulder to keep from making more noise than she already was, but it didn't do much to muffle the groans that came from her mouth as Aaron thrust into her. Serena wrapped her legs around him, pulling him harder into her as she arched her back and pushed up against him. When her body tensed, he knew she was about to come, and he fucked her faster, listening for the telltale exhalation of breath that told him she'd reached her peak. When it came, he let go, fucking her wildly, mounting toward his own orgasm until he came, pulsing deep inside her as her pussy spasmed around his thrusting cock. When he sighed and sank down, spent, on top of her, she coiled her arms around him and plucked the blindfold off his face.

"See?" Serena cooed. "I told you I'd saved you a plate."

"It makes me want to be late every year," said Aaron.

"Don't you dare," she said. "Besides, there's still pumpkin pie."

"With whipped cream?"

Serena smiled.

"You know it."

"But I've already had my dessert."

"Tough," she said, her lips against his ear. "You're having some more."

Even Aaron couldn't argue with logic like that.

Hunger
by Emilie Paris

You want it but you can't have it.

This concept is my favorite form of sexual torture. It's why I like being tied down, why I fantasize about people who are out of my reach. I am fascinated by the erotica of denial, of hunger as an aphrodisiac. Yes, I ultimately succumb to my cravings, but I wallow in the euphoria of holding out as long as possible. Denying myself makes the first bite, lick, or taste that much sweeter. Who doesn't crave the forbidden – be it food or fantasy?

What food is forbidden? Not apples, of course. Not since Eve. Not anymore. But sweets. The seductive dark, sticky treats. Sugar-glazed and rich in butter, dripping with icing and freshly whipped cream. And what X-rated acts are forbidden? The same sort, of course. The type you crave late at night, when you've exhausted all of the many possibilities on cable. Images bubble up in your mind, unplanned, unwanted, unexpected. If you give into them, you might never be able to get back. *That's* the fear that binds me to the good-girl track.

Denial, I remind myself. *Hunger, as an aphrodisiac.*

It's my mantra. It keeps me in place. At least, it does so until the urges become too strong to ignore, and I'm forced to dress, hurriedly, to make my way to the car, to drive out on the empty streets until I reach his house. (Who can explain why desires are always so much stronger at night?) I knock on the door, just loudly enough to make him hear me. And then I stand there, head down, and wait for what I know he has to say.

"No, baby. No."

At his words, that unquenchable yearning overwhelms me and makes me fall on my knees on his porch, desperate. He is the man who has drenched me in chocolate. Who has squeezed the juice of the ripest berries over my naked skin. He is the man who has taught me to eat at his feet, mouth open, waiting, hungry. The one who has made me so fucking hungry.

I've been good for so long, I think to myself. I've denied myself for so long. I need to devour a feast – not of food, but of him. And I don't mean simply sex – but the dirtiest, stickiest sort of sex, dripping with icing, sugar-glazed. Rich, too rich to handle.

"Please," I say, knowing how it sounds and how it looks. Here I am, again, in the middle of the night, on his porch, and he and I both know that I'll do anything to make him take pity on me.

"Baby," he says softly, "No."

I think of the weeks that have gone by since I last had him inside me. I think of the crazy cravings that keep me up late at night, cravings that I try to control with thoughts of why the two of us can't be together. And all the reasons that sound so good and honest and smart in the daytime, fade to nothing when I am hungry for him. One of us has to be strong. Is that right? One of us has to be the one who stays together, who remains unmoved.

But not tonight.

I shake my head, muttering under my breath, almost

like a crazy person. I'm not crazy. I'm hungry. That's what I say, looking up at him and realizing somehow that he was waiting for me. It's three a.m., but he's not in his sweats. I didn't wake him up. He's in jeans and a T-shirt and I can tell by the way he's staring at me, that he was wide awake before I came wrapping at his door. He was awake and thinking of me, and that's what gives me the edge.

I smile, because it's almost as if I can smell the sex now, smell the scent of our sex and how good it will feel and how fulfilled I will be. I smile, and shake my head, because I know he's taunting me by keeping me out here in the chill pre-dawn air, but that he's going to give in. He's as out of his head with yearning as I am. His cock is as hard in his jeans as my pussy is wet. I lick my bottom lip when I look at the bulge in his slacks.

"Let me in –"

"You shouldn't be here."

So he's right. So fucking what. "Shouldn't" doesn't mean anything to me right now. "Shouldn't" is like a made-up word that has no translation into my language. I reach forward, and he steps away.

Denial, I think. *Hunger as an aphrodisiac.*

The words have lost their magical power. I can't hold myself back. My desire is too strong. I sigh as I remember everything he and I have done together. Oh, we've been dirty. We've played with olive oil, with butter, with icing. We've played with ripe fruits and slippery vegetables. With eggs. With wine. With everything. We've been the messiest of lovers and now we're tangled in a mess that's far worse than any kitchen disaster we could have created ourselves. And truly I don't give a fuck. Because without him, I can't eat and I can't sleep and I can't even think straight. And I know

144

somehow that it's the same for him.

"I'm so hungry," I say, and he shakes his head once more, but I know I'm going to dine tonight. I know that my appetite will be momentarily satiated when he reaches for my hand and leads me into the apartment.

Dear Alison
by Maxim Jakubowski

Dear Alison,

Last fall, two CD tributes to Kris Kristofferson were released at almost the same time on different small labels. Both featured a motley assortment of country and Americana artists with their interpretations of, mostly, the same classic songs. It reminded me that I first came across Kristofferson as an actor in a much underrated film called *Cisco Pike*, which also featured his music, if my memory serves me right. And all these years later, I'm no longer even sure of that. Suffice to say, I loved the man and his music and, notwithstanding the fact than I am junkie music consumer, naturally had to buy both the CDs.

The opening track on "Don't Let The Bastards Get You Down" is a version of a rather obscure KK song called 'The Hawk' by Tom Verlaine. Tom Verlaine used to be the voice and main guitar player (Richard Lloyd was the other) in the neo-punk group Television, whose 'Marquee Moon' has ruled many of my air guitar daydreams ever since. Sadly one hears very little of Verlaine these days (and the same goes for Kris Kristofferson too).

I'm just recovering from a serious bout of flu and had been laid low by the bug for almost a week, losing a stone or so along with my appetite and much of my energy. Not that I'm using this as an excuse for not having submitted the 'erotic fruit' story I had promised you a month ago. To cut a long story short, my mood had been so low I had barely been able to listen to music during my illness, let alone write, work or concentrate much on anything bar reading entertainment magazines or feeling nauseous at the sheer thought of food.

Tom Verlaine's mournful voice is an acquired taste, even for me such a fan of melancholy notes in Leonard Cohen and other singers but his guitar playing is something else. And listening to this song which opens the tribute CD awakened me to life again. Such is the power of music. The barely there, hesitant vocals underpinned by crystal like, ever so slow guitar arpeggios with a beauty and an economy I just cannot describe but that somehow gave me hope again that one day, in a story or a future book, I could attain just such beauty, such epiphany. Verlaine's guitar, Carla Torgerson of the Walkabouts' voice, sometimes Springsteen at his saddest. Oh yes, Alison, there is redemption in this world. Bliss.

But no story about fruit, I fear.

I had an idea when I wrote you last, but somehow it didn't gell. Did I ever warn you that I'm actually not that good writing on a particular theme, even if I've edited quite a few books of the kind myself (but the eager literary detective will quickly establish the fact those are usually the ones in which I don't force feed a story of my own)? Oh, I know the reason well, mind you. On one hand I'm not that disciplined enough; on the other, it's just that I don't have much imagination actually. For years now, much of my fiction has been about myself, under various guises, costumes, incarnations, alter egos and assorted subterfuges which I'm deeply convinced so many people can see right through and when I completed my last novel (blandly lying to questions and interviews that it was in fact my least autobiographical when in fact it was anything but; ah, aren't post-modernism and metafiction wonderful alibis?) I firmly decided that it would represent the end of that era and that my next book would be a total work of the imagination. After all, what with my imperfect life and the risks I've been taking for too many years now, surely one day my wife and others would begin to read through the lines better and there was no smoke without fire and all that.

And, having resolved to change my bad pseudo confessional habits, I promptly conjured up a great title for the new book which I pitched to my publisher and now he has it scheduled and I still have no idea whatsoever what the novel is going to be about (but, yes, it is going to be different from my previous ones; has to be) and I sit here paralysed and unable to settle on an opening line. I'd hoped writing this little story you'd asked for would unblock me. I really did. But, fruit? As unoriginal as I usually am, I just can't descend to the obvious level of bananas and cucumbers, surely? Although I'm sure many of your other contributors will (and no doubt admirably transcend the innate vulgarity of the fruit in question). You see, I've only used fruit in a sexual context once. And, for a damn change, I'm now reluctant to tell the story. In a way, I've betrayed so many women I've been with, had sex with, fucked, used, whatever terminology you prefer to use, in my writing already that you'd reckon one final indiscretion now would make no difference. But something in me wants to turn a new leaf. I really do.

KC, when she read the stories in which I featured her, send me a sad note accusing me of describing her, her sublime white body, her face, her cunt, her slightly out of kilter teeth, her heartbreaking small smile, like meat. I was shocked. All I had been trying to do at the time was evoke the sheer beauty of her, of my love for her, even if it was adulterous (and maybe engineer her return through the magic of my feelings transmuted into words; little did I know that the randomness of the alphabet just has no power to awaken feelings anew).

I should have learned my lesson there and then.

But did I ever say I was wise? In fact, I sometimes feel that I grow more foolish as I grow older.

I'm drawn to risk, to other women, to sex. They're just there, you see. Sometimes just out of reach of course but at other times I somehow do find the right repartee, wry smile and I plunge headlong into yet another affair. Sometimes at night, I rationalize that maybe what I am really seeking is the blinding nova that was KC in my life, but I'm kidding myself. They have all been so different from her. Dark haired, auburn, ash blonde, every colour under the sun that she was not. Every shape and taste other than hers. Maybe I don't even remember the name of every woman I've been with since then, but I do recall the varied hotel rooms and the mechanics, the ballet of sex, the moans, the fears, the sighs and breaths taken. And … oh, the eyes when she peers in your soul as she comes, your cock still embedded inside her or your tongue or teeth on her clitoral jewel …

New York: Algonquin, Iroquois, Gershwin, Washington Square hotels. Paris: St Thomas d' Aquin, Bersolys, de l'Odeon, des Ecoles. Sete: Grand Hotel. New Orleans: Burgundy, St Pierre, Sheraton. Seattle:

Stouffer, In on Pike. San Diego: Handlery. Amsterdam: Krasnapolsky, Singel. Los Angeles: Figueroa, Pasadena Hilton. Chicago: Hilton Towers, Drake, Inn on Grant Park. The list goes on. Which I bequeath to future divorce lawyers.

I have been a serial lover. By habit and conviction. Guilty to the last degree. Sometimes I was even juggling several affairs. But somehow I never got the names mixed up in moments of passion or my itineraries confused. Even now, as my long-distance relationship with CC in Germany moves into its second year and to unheard of levels of intimacy (we've progressed beyond hotel rooms and I've actually spent nights in her actual bed, in the apartment which she shares with her teenage son who sleeps in the room down the corridor), I am still hopeful of reviving the embers of the great sex I had with AK (who, for a change, really got a thrill from featuring in a story and a book of mine; although her erstwhile boyfriend didn't appreciate it the same way but then he was a fool for allowing her to stray) and am even curiously flirting with JR, who works in marketing just around the corner from my office and has a nice smile and a spark in her eyes, or maybe I'm misinterpreting the vibrations. Somehow I'm always open to suggestions, my eye roving liberally around the myriad possibilities (I even allowed my wickedness to wonderingly admire your own photo on the back of your last book cover and briefly checked your bio) and my mind weaving absurd but so enjoyable webs of seduction, even if my body is these days unlikely to follow suit (weakened by the bug, in bed the other morning, my penis had never looked so shrivelled ...).

So why am I now all so suddenly shy to tell you my raspberry story, or any rate couch it in fictional guise?

Yes, that was the fruit involved. It was an affair that only lasted a few days in New York and then we parted ways by common agreement, she back to Australia, me back to London, talk about the safety of distance. She was a writer there who had submitted a story to me which I'd liked, published and we'd begun to correspond and one thing had slowly led to another. But enough of the story of my rather brief involvement with CF.

The thought occurred while writing you this long letter of apology for the non-appearance of my story that, even if I had a better imagination than the muse provided me with, I'm no longer sure that fruit is truly inspiring or even erotic. Now, food would have been another kettle of fish altogether! I love food. No reservations whatsoever. There was a section in a newspaper colour supplement here recently about sex and food which just made my lips wet, text and illustrations all. Did you know there is a restaurant in Tokyo, which has now opened a branch in Manchester in which you can dine off a naked woman's body? The recumbent naked woman is clothed only in strategically placed scallop shells and whatever you've ordered for supper. Not a new idea I know; the surrealists used it. However, the sensual quality of the UK version is restricted somewhat by the use of Cling film (do you call that Saran Wrap in America, I think?) as a hygienic barrier between skin and the diner. But you can replicate the Tokyo experience at home: take one naked woman (men aren't appropriate, since food items can be lost in chest hair). Adorn with sushi, sashimi or other cold foodstuff. Do not try this with, say, sausage, potato mash and a rich onion gravy. You'll make a hell of a mess, and the gravy could be a scalding liability. Offer to wash up that night though.

Of course, beyond the parameters of taste, we all

know since Mickey Rourke and Kim Basinger in 9 1/2 (or do you recall *Tom Jones'* gastronomy-plus highlights?) that food and sex form an exquisite galaxy of erotic possibilities. Spaghetti dangling precariously between plate and mouth, cherries slowly penetrating the barrier of lips in a symphony of red and scarlet (oh, a fruit; hadn't somehow occurred to me until right now ...), asparagus, the stiletto of the legume world, ice cream, chocolate of all kinds. Now, if you want to one day put together an anthology of sex and food, Alison, count me in and I will not fail you again. Oysters and New Orleans; yes, that's what I'd write about and let your fertile imagination improvise on that one you wicked woman ... There are some who say libertines don't mix sex and food; they reason that before sex, libertines concentrate on one thing. At that moment, sex is their only obsession. Also they need to keep their bodies light. I beg to disagree. Tell that to the Romans who were partial to some vestal virgins or even common whores feeding grapes into open throats before the traditional orgy. Tut, tut, grapes, another fruit I'd hitherto neglected!

With food involved, I'd be in fine form. From the wonderful excesses of Marco Ferreri's excesses in his movie LA GRANDE BOUFFE to the pornographic delights of sashimi slices against pale flesh, yellow-tail tuna shades contrasting with the rainbow of variations a nipple can move through in the throes of passion, let alone arousal, I just wouldn't know where to stop, you know. Actually, CF's nipples in New York were delightfully dark, as were her labia. The Gershwin Hotel, corner of 27th and 5th, it was, a Picasso sketch drawn across the far wall overseeing our frolics or was it Matisse? Sorry for my confusion, I also took a Cincinnati bank female executive to that particular hotel some years later, so the precise details are a touch unclear.

OK, so I'll tell you what actually happened. Satisfied?

It's not enough of a story to make a story, you'll surely agree.

We'd agreed to meet up in New York. A suitably halfway place as any, I suppose. I think that from the moment we lay eyes on each other at Newark Airport, we both realized that the attraction that had undeniably existed over letters, telephone and a perfunctory exchange of photographs, hers nude, mine clothed, was not going to translate that well into the arena of the bed. But we had committed to the escapade and we couldn't afford to get an extra hotel room. The sex had been poor the first couple of days. Lack of conviction and fire from both of us, no doubt. It was mechanical. As if we'd been married for years already. She was one of my first extracurricular women since KC and she was still in recovery from the break-up of her first affair since her husband had left her for another man. You could say we were still beginners in the subtle art of the zipless fuck. Somehow, she didn't mind me fucking her, touching her everywhere, my fingers entering all her holes but she refused to take my cock in her mouth. I've never felt that fellatio was obligatory or necessarily pleasurable to receive but the simple fact she denied me this annoyed me intensely (reminded of Maryann, an American blonde I had known in my early twenties in Paris, who would allow me to do absolutely anything to her, including fucking her mouth, but would scream if I even touched her nipples by accident; you always yearn for what is denied you …).

Between fucks, we'd explore Manhattan and the Village together and our lively conversation would conjure up in daring scenarios which might spice up our times together. She wanted me to pick up another girl and invite her to join us (a fantasy that, unlike many other men, had never turned me on) but I failed abysmally in my feeble attempts to connect with another woman in the bars I trawled that afternoon while CF did some shopping. Possibly the inner knowledge that I was disappointing to CF, sexually, intellectually, detracted from my attraction to others, let alone identifying or convincing one who was also bisexual. It was winter and I was surprised to see a Korean 24 hour deli on University Place selling small raspberry punnets at that time of year and decided to treat myself and brought a couple. They were even reasonably priced.

Back at the hotel, I greedily downed the first batch on my own and set aside the remaining. At the time, I had no other ulterior motive. I swear. When I travel I always keep some chocolate in the bedside drawer. The sugar rush always helps me wake in the morning when my mouth is pasty and dry. On this occasion I recall with utter precision it was a few bars of Lindt, praline filled squares, which I'd picked up at Heathrow while waiting in line in the food hall of the departure lounge to pay for my breakfast sandwich and Coca-Cola. I casually put the remaining raspberries in the same drawer.

When CF returned to the room later, she didn't even question me about my vain efforts to find a third party. She seemed in a better mood than the morning. Maybe the time spent without me had been good for her. We dined at a nearby Japanese place and missed out on the final movie performances at the Union Square multiplex. Back in the room, we undressed and she initiated the first kiss before we had even slipped between the bed sheets. This was a first. I had until now had to make the first sexual step.

Fifteen minutes later, she separated from a particularly tender embrace and, unbidden, went down on me. Things were certainly on the up. She sucked very well, a consummate expert with lips, tongue, whole mouth and a delicate occasional use of teeth even, slow, methodical, rhythmic. I abandoned myself to her ministrations. Maybe this was going to work after all?

Later, having moved into a 69 position and studiously attempting to pleasure her in turn, I marvelled again at the subtle, dark hue of her outer labia and was reminded of the evening I had borrowed KC's lipstick and used it on the outer perimeter of her cunt to highlight the entrance to my then gate of paradise (I'd also darkened her perilously pale nipples and licked her clean but that's another story which I've too often told before and which ain't going to bring her back).

"Stay like that," I'd asked CF, detaching myself from her.

She lazily acquiesced. By now, we had somehow reached a situation of quiet trust and sexual complicity.

I stretched my arm over to the bedside drawer and pulled out a handful of raspberries.

CF followed my movement.

"What are you doing?" she asked.

"Shhh …"

I dimmed the light and squeezed a few raspberries between my fingers, mashing them together, the ensuing juice trickling steadily down my wrist and onto her stomach. I spread the red liquid down to her cunt and adorned her private lips, the dark red enhanced the brown hue of her folds and highlighted the wetness peering through her opening.

"Kinky," she remarked.

"You think so?"

I began to lick her moistness, her strong taste now blending with the acid of the mashed fruit. Then a mad thought flashed through my mind and without missing a tongue twist I extended my left arm again to the bedside and pulled out a couple of the chocolate squares and quickly inserted them into her cunt . Within seconds, the heat of her insides had melted it and it slowly began to sip through her cunt lips. I took hold of the remaining raspberries and carefully crushed them into pulp then pushed the gooey remains of the fruit into her with almost all of my hand, past the feeble barrier of her lips and the sticky, pliant wall of liquid chocolate bubbling there like volcano lava.

"Hmmm …" CF gasped. "So what now? Are you going to eat me or fuck me?" she asked wickedly.

I fucked her.

Never had a cunt felt so hot and dirty and welcoming to my cock. I came quickly. Then couldn't resist lowering myself down to her ploughed entrance again to taste myself within the leaking residue of raspberry and chocolate seeping out of her, drop by lingering drop.

"Look, you're making the bed all filthy …" CF remarked, pointing down to my detumescing cock, dangling brown trails on the white sheet beneath us. So she sucked me off again. Sucked me clean, and I'm being literal, not vulgar.

There you are. Jakubowski's raspberry story. This is a true story. Do not try this at home.

CF and I parted friends and we still e-mail each other a few times a year. After me, she had a long affair back in Sydney with another woman but right now she appears to be happily into another heterosexual relationship, with a man who doesn't mind her having two grown-up children. She hasn't submitted me any stories since, though.

I never considered stuffing raspberries up a lover's cunt again, or maybe it was that I did not see any on sale at nearby stores when visiting strange cities with other lovers. I once tried to insert chocolate into AK but she didn't like it one iota. Was fearful of infection. Stated that her inside walls were too sensitive. Anyway, wouldn't have been the same without the magic ingredient: fresh raspberries …

So, Alison, this is a secret between you and me. A future bond, maybe? A secret I gift you to compensate for the fact I have not been able to let you have a new short story on the theme of sex and fruit for your anthology. Hope it makes you smile, at least and I'm confident the book will do well without one of my feeble self-centered efforts. Good luck.

By the way, what is your favorite fruit, and what is/was your relationship to it? I promise I won't tell.

Warmly,
Maxim J.

Hot Tomato
by Oscar Shemoth

Ever since it got hot this summer, you've started gardening wearing almost nothing. A long T-shirt with no pants; the one-piece you wear to swim; shorts with no top; sometimes just your bra and panties. Once I caught you gardening naked, and that made you blush. You always wash yourself off with the garden hose before you come back inside, dripping on the floor, your skin moist and steamy with the heat and the moisture. Recently your arms have been bundled with zucchini, squash, carrots.

Now, it's finally tomato season.

You've got on your red string bikini, the one you wear to sunbathe. There's not much to it; it's nothing more than a string between your cheeks, and in the front it hangs so low I can see a hint of your pubic hair. If you wore it outside the back yard, you'd have to shave, I think. On top it clings to your breasts awkwardly, looking like at any moment it's going to fall away into nothing. It's bright red. Tomato red.

I watch you from the patio, reclining on a chaise lounge with an ice-cold bloody mary. I watch you on your hands and knees, checking tomatoes and picking the ones that are ripe. Bending far forward, so far forward that I can see the lips of your sex spreading around the thin string of your bikini bottoms. So far forward that I can see your upper body from between your legs, your nipples popping out of the bikini top as you pluck a tomato from a plant. I lick the vodka-and-Tabasco-spiked tomato taste from a celery stalk and wonder if your pussy tastes like tomatoes when you've been picking them all day.

You straighten, bundling the fruits of your labour in your arms awkwardly, reaching behind you to pluck the string from between your cheeks, perhaps not even realizing that I could see your lips. You adjust the top, tucking your nipples away. The bright red bikini contrasts against your rich, tanned skin. I start to get hard.

You come back toward the house with your arms filled with tomatoes, pausing only to turn on the garden hose and spray water over your muddy knees and feet, washing them clean so that your tanned skin glistens. Water splashes up and moistens your bikini top, making it even more transparent, making it cling more firmly to the shape of you. Your face is a mask of elation, your eyes bright with enthusiasm as you rush toward the kitchen.

"You won't believe the taste of these tomatoes," you gush.

My eyes linger on your full, ripe breasts, nipples distending the red material of your top. I smile at you.

"I can hardly wait," I say.

You disappear into the kitchen, your cheeks bouncing ripe as I glance back after you. I have to readjust my shorts to keep my cock from pressing painfully against them. I sip the bloody mary and taste the sharp vodka and hot sauce camouflaging the taste of tomato.

You come out a few minutes later with the cutting board, ripe tomatoes sliced and laid out. You're also holding glass of water. "You *have* to try these," you say, your breasts almost popping out of your bikini top as you come around and kneel by my chaise lounge.

"I want to try them," I say.

"Here," you tell me, handing me the water. "Clean your palate. Swish it around. You've got to have a clean palate."

"My palate is anything but clean," I say.

"I know. Drink the water."

I drink half the glass and swish the water around my mouth, washing away the taste of the bloody mary.

"Now close your eyes," you tell me.

I close them and open my mouth.

"Just taste," you say, and place a tomato slice on my tongue like a bikini-clad priest disbursing the holy communion.

The tomato is still hot from the sun. The taste is hearty, rich. The bite of citrus is followed by a rush of smoky taste – pure musk.

"Doesn't it just taste like sex?" you giggle.

I open my eyes, look into yours, let my glance flicker down over your body, its ripe rounded curves full and pink with the sun.

"Yes," I say. "It tastes exactly like sex."

"Okay," you say. "Here, drink more water and close your eyes."

I obey, opening my mouth.

"This is a different variety," you tell me. "This is an heirloom."

"You don't say."

This one, also warm, is faintly spicy, the taste pulsing hot through my tongue before the musky bouquet hits me. It's spicy enough that it surprises me, burning just a little as it goes down.

"Now that one <u>really</u> tastes like sex," I say.

"I know," you tell me, smiling as I open my eyes.

One breast has come free from the skimpy red bikini top; your nipple pokes out just over the edge.

I drink more water, take the cutting board away from you and set it on the little metal table.

Then I grab your shoulders.

"What are you doing?" you ask.

"Dirtying my palate," I say, and push you onto the chaise lounge as I slide out of it.

You're giggling as I reach for your bottoms You don't even protest that the neighbours might see – any neighbour still watching wants to see whatever he or she can. You struggle a little getting into the chaise lounge, but you don't protest. I get my fingers under the string of your bikini bottoms and pull them down quickly.

Your face is flushed with the sun and with the taste of sex. You tuck your breasts back into the bikini top.

"Oh no you don't," I say, and I reach up and pull the top down.

My hands caress your ripe tomatoes as my mouth descends between your parted thighs. The memory of the tomato's musk complements your taste, and it fills my mouth as I reach out with one hand and seize a warm tomato slice, popping it into your mouth.

You moan faintly around the crushed pulp of the tomato. Red juice runs down your chin.

My tongue slides between your lips and I taste that you're wet – so wet juice runs down my chin, too. I put another tomato slice in your mouth as my tongue finds your clit, and your tomato-muffled moan rises in volume.

Then you're quiet, laying back in the chaise lounge

and panting softly as I caress your clit with my tongue.

When I slip another tomato slice into your mouth you seize my fingers and suckle them, coating them with tomato juice. It runs down my wrist and dribbles onto your round, bare breasts. I press my tongue harder against your clit and your back arches.

Tomato juice dribbles down your neck and joins the juice already coating your breasts, soaking the bikini. Lucky it's red. Your moans rise in volume and pitch, and you're very close to coming.

I've got your right on the edge when I lift my face from your pussy, pull down my shorts, and climb onto the chaise lounge with you.

Your eyes are closed in rapture, your mouth hanging halfway open, your lips slicked with juice. I put another slice on your tongue and you suckle it hungrily as my lips press to yours, my tongue delving in to the taste of tomato and of you. My cock finds your lips and eases neatly between them. You're so wet I don't have to wait.

You come almost as soon as I enter you, moaning into my mouth, your breaths then coming fast and short as I suck the tomato pulp out of your mouth and savour it hungrily. I fuck you fast, my hands on your breasts, squeezing gently. You're still thrashing and whimpering in orgasm when I come, letting out a thunderous moan and plunging deep inside you as my cock explodes. I slump onto you, licking the juice from the underside of your throat.

"Don't you love tomato season?" you ask.

"I love every season," I tell you. "Just wait until the squash is ready."

Good Fortune
by Scott Wallace

"I'm famished," said Ivy as Adam pulled her chair out for her.

"I'm glad," said Adam, taking his own seat. "This is the best Chinese restaurant in town. I recommend the Peking Duck."

Ivy looked around, plainly impressed by the lavish surroundings. Shoji screens with images of swans, sunrises, clouds and bamboo trees were scattered around the restaurant, suffusing it with a gentle, soothing light. The scent of finely prepared Chinese delicacies was intoxicating. The waiter, clad in a white tuxedo, approached with their menus.

"Something to drink for the lady?" he asked.

"House red?" said Ivy, peering over the menu.

"The same for me," said Adam.

"Very good," said the waiter, and placed a tray in front of Ivy. The tray held a single fortune cookie.

Ivy looked up at the waiter, but he had vanished around the twists and turns of the shoji screens. "What's this?" she asked, picking up the fortune cookie and peering quizzically at Adam.

"I don't know," said Adam innocently. "You'd better open it."

"How did he know I love fortune cookies?"

"Ancient Chinese secret," said Adam. "Open the cookie."

Ivy cracked open the fortune cookie and began eating it, savouring the crisp, sweet morsels.

"You're not reading the fortune," said Adam.

"It's an old superstition I have," said Ivy. "You can't read the fortune until after you've eaten the cookie."

"Good thing you like fortune cookies."

"But I usually don't eat them at the start of a meal." Ivy munched the last bits of fortune cookie and unfurled the tiny white slip of paper.

She turned several shades of pink, then red. She looked up at Adam and then back down again. Her date was smiling enigmatically.

"Well?" he asked.

"Well what?" said Ivy meekly, too embarrassed to look her date in the eye.

"Well?" said Adam.

Ivy was dressed in a little white cocktail number that, Adam thought, looked incredible on her. It was skimpy in all the right places, cut just low enough to display a hint of cleavage and a fetching swell where Ivy's slim breasts tented the material. He could see the spray of pale lace at the neckline where her bra peeked over. As Adam watched, Ivy's nipples grew visible through the thin white material.

Ivy looked up at Adam, blushing more fiercely than ever. She looked down again, embarrassed, then up again, locking eyes with him. Her nipples became still more visible, and Adam couldn't resist a glance at them even as Ivy was watching. He and Ivy hadn't slept

164

together yet, though it was pretty clear they were going to. Imagining the sight of those small pink nipples, taunting himself with the thought of their taste and feel against his tongue, brought Adam's cock to full mast in silk Armani suit pants.

Ivy's pale cleavage blushed as red as her face, and she clutched the tiny slip of paper like a waif with a $100 bill.

"Well?" repeated Adam.

Ivy unclenched her hand and looked down at the slip of paper.

It said "TAKE OFF YOUR PANTIES."

"Well." said Adam, and this time it wasn't a question.

Her face hot, her breath coming short, Ivy looked around the restaurant and shifted in her seat, nudging herself closer to the table. They were in the middle of the room, and while the shoji screens presented some cover, they were nowhere near a wall.

Ivy's hands crept up her thighs, lifting the hem of her skirt up above the lace tops of her white stockings. She felt so wicked for having put a white lace thong on over her garters – but she'd imagined that tonight was the night she and Adam would finally sleep together, and she wanted to impress him with her worldly knowledge and brazen sexiness.

That had certainly backfired. Now Adam was watching her blush, a smile on his face, plainly enjoying the way in which he'd embarrassed her.

But Ivy was enjoying it too. Her nipples were so hard they hurt. Her stomach was doing flip flops. She knew when she took off her panties they would be wet.

She eased her hands up under her dress and snugged down the thin white lace of her thong. She looked around nervously, but no one seemed to be noticing her. She eased her panties down her thighs, hoping that the clean white tablecloth provided just enough cover for her to get away with this. She brought her panties down past her knees, then over her calves and dropped them to the floor. She lifted first one high-heeled shoe and then the other, and bent down as if picking up a dropped fork. She tucked the panties in her handbag, and her gaze zeroed back in on Adam, who was smiling.

But not before she noticed that her thong was, indeed, soaked through.

"May I take your order?" asked the waiter as he set down their wine.

"Oh," said Ivy. "I haven't even had a chance to look at the menu. Can ... can we have a minute?"

"Certainly," said the waiter, and deposited another tray in front of the blushing Ivy.

Ivy looked at Adam, her clit throbbing painfully between her tightly clenched thighs. So aware was she of her lack of underwear that every time she shifted in her chair she felt a surge of arousal.

Adam nodded toward the fortune cookie.

Ivy broke it open, staring into Adam's dark eyes as she ate the cookie in small pieces, savouring the sweet, crunchy crumb. She clutched the second fortune desperately, afraid to look.

"Read it," said Adam.

Ivy opened her palm, finding the second fortune damp with her sweat. The first fortune was translucent with moisture. She read the second and couldn't stifle a tiny moan that escaped her lips. Her eyes seemed to cross, her head spinning.

"Read it," said Adam softly. "Out loud."

"It says –" she began, and stopped, her throat tight. Ivy took a deep breath, then looked into Adam's eyes.

Her face pinkened further and she swallowed. Her mouth felt sticky with the sweet of the fortune cookie. Her pussy throbbed as she tried to find her voice, the filthy sentence grasping her even as she longed to say it.

"It says –" she started again, and couldn't go on.

Finally, she leaned across the table, bringing her face close to Adam's, and he leaned close as well.

Ivy whispered: "It says, 'Finger your pussy and tell me how wet you are.'"

"Then you'd better do that," said Adam.

Glancing around, Ivy nervously let her thighs slip a few inches a part. Snuggling her hand gently under her skirt, she touched her cunt and felt a sudden flush of excitement as its juices dribbled onto the tips of her fingers. She removed her hand and leaned close again.

Adam looked at her and shook his head.

"It said, 'finger,' not 'touch'," he told Ivy, and her clit gave a surge.

Her eyes roving the restaurant to make sure no one was watching, Ivy drew her hand back up her thigh. She snuck it under her skirt and pressed it firmly against her sex, having to spread her thighs further to gain access. She put one finger in and gasped, feeling like she was going to pass out.

She leaned very close to Adam and said, "I'm very wet."

"How wet?" asked Adam.

"Incredibly wet," whispered Ivy.

"Wet enough to get fucked?"

"More than that," she blushed, her voice soft and husky with desire.

"Enjoying your wine?" asked the waiter, his smile tantalizing as he stood beside them with a pad ready and a tray tucked to one side.

"Oh, God," said Ivy before she could silence herself. Her eyes remained riveted on the tray with its single fortune cookie.

"I think we'll have the Peking Duck," said Adam. "And we'll start with an order of pot stickers, some egg rolls and the hot and sour soup."

"Very good," said the waiter, jotting the order down. He placed the tray before Ivy and left.

Ivy looked at Adam, hunger in her gaze, her hand shaking.

"Read it," said Adam, standing up. "I'm going to use the restroom."

Ivy cracked open the cookie and ate one crumb, then another, savouring each morsel as she stared at the white slip of paper without reading it. Finally, she let the fragments of fortune cookie fall to the white tablecloth and read the fortune without finishing the cookie.

She took a deep, slow breath, shifting nervously in her seat.

The fortune said: "YOU WILL HAVE SEX WITH A HANDSOME STRANGER IN A CHINESE RESTAURANT'S MEN'S ROOM."

Ivy stood up, her knees shaking. She left her purse, panties, and all, tucked under the table. She walked on unsteady legs toward the back of the restaurant, picking up speed with each table she passed.

By the time she reached the long corridor that led to the restrooms, she was practically sprinting.

Adam was waiting for her with the light turned off. As she slipped into the men's room, he grabbed her and pulled her deeper into the jasmine-scented darkness, slamming her against the door so that her behind forced it shut even as Adam crushed her to the door with his weight. A moan escaped Ivy's lips in the instant before

168

he kissed her, his tongue tasting the fortune-cookie sweetness of her mouth. He gently pushed her legs apart and drew his fingers up her slit, feeling for himself how wet she was. Ivy regained her senses and began to claw hungrily at Adam's belt, her hands shaking so bad it took her three tries to get his zipper down. By then, Adam had unzipped the back of her dress and pulled it forward. She shrugged it over her shoulder and down her arms. Taking Adam's cock into her hands and stroking it hungrily as he unclasped her bra and brought his mouth first to one hard nipple, then to the other, suckling them. Ivy dropped to her knees, Adam's tongue leaving a slick trail up her neck. She took his cock in her mouth and sucked hungrily, moaning low in her throat as her lips slid up and down the shaft.

Adam leaned hard against the door, his hands caressing her face as she sucked him. She looked up at him but she could see absolutely nothing – just darkness. Adam took her shoulders and lifted her up. He took firm hold of her and turned her around, pushing her gently forward into blackness. Her dress went sliding over her shoulders and past her hips and down her slim legs. She stepped out of it, not even caring that it was now on the restroom floor. She shrugged off her bra and Adam eased her against the sink, bending her over. Her breasts pushed against the cold porcelain and she gasped. Ivy let him spread her legs wide. His cock, still moist from her mouth, nudged open her pussy lips.

Ivy stifled a moan of pleasure as Adam entered her. She gripped the sink and stifled another moan, this one with much greater difficulty, as he pushed all the way into her and reached under to stroke her clit. Then she couldn't stifle her moans at all – they were erupting, uncontrolled, from her wide-open mouth, as Adam fucked her deep and rubbed her clit quickly. She came almost right away, and began pushing herself back onto Adam's cock even as his other hand caressed her nipples and covered her small breasts. Soon she knew she was going to come again, and she reached her second climax just as Adam bit the back of her neck, hard, almost as hard as she liked it, making her squeal with hunger as he pumped into her. Ivy gripped the porcelain sink, her ass raised high and her legs spread to take Adam's thrusting cock as he sighed warmly into her ear, emptying his cock deep into her clenching, hungry cunt.

When he drew his cock back out of her, Ivy trembled hard against the sink. Adam helped her back into her dress in the dark, not bothering with her bra, which he tucked into the pocket of his suit jacket. He guided Ivy to the door and she slipped out into the restaurant, hair mussed, face pink. Her pussy felt wet and filled as she walked back to the table and sat down, her head swirling.

The appetizers and soup were waiting for her. The waiter had swept away the fragments of her last, unfinished cookie, along with the three slips of paper.

Adam joined her a moment later.

"Eat up," he said. "You said you were famished."

"I ... I don't seem to be hungry any more," said Ivy, her voice hoarse from moaning. She looked up at Adam and smiled sheepishly.

Adam's dark eyes seized her, and his own mouth twitched in a wicked smile.

"Those fortune cookies can be filling," said Adam.

Ivy took a deep breath, closed her eyes and sighed.

"Yes," she said. "They certainly can."

Cherry Slushee
by Alison Tyler

I don't know how I get myself into situations like this. None of my girlfriends ever seem to find themselves in such unusual positions. I guess I have a knack. A knack for getting myself into the stickiest sort of trouble. Of course, none of my girlfriends seem to have as much good sex as I do, so maybe the two go hand in hand – or hand in handcuff, or whatever.

Perhaps, the real problem is just that I stay up way too late. When you're wide-eyed in the wee hours of the morning, your judgement can become impaired. Small circumstances take on large meaning. Everything depends on how the shadows play, on the shift and sway of car headlights dancing across a darkened wall.

The thing was that I'd just gotten my own apartment, had only started to learn about living on my own. I thought there would be a huge enlightenment, or some sort of awakening that went with living solo. And there was. An awakening, anyway. The main change in my life was that I no longer slept regular hours. Being on my own meant I could stay up and paint all night if I wanted to, and that's what I ended up doing. Painting from ten at night until five in the morning, and then heading out to

171

the local 24-hour grocery store to pick up breakfast foods and coffee. Often, I wouldn't crash until sometime late in the afternoon. I loved it. Despite the purple circles occasionally darkening the pale skin beneath my eyes. Despite the fact that I couldn't manage to do brunch with friends any longer and they started referring to me as "the vampire." To me, living alone equalled freedom, and freedom meant not living – or sleeping – by anyone else's schedule.

And that's how I got myself in such a sticky situation. By not sleeping. But sticky can be good. That's what my brunch-loving friends don't realize. Sticky can be sweet, much sweeter than being clean, and washed, and sliding in between the sheets at a quarter to eleven. Sticky can be much more exciting than having to wake up every morning at half-past six.

I was pretty sure I wasn't the only one who felt this way. There was a handsome checker at the grocery who seemed to like working odd hours. He watched me whenever I went running in for my post-midnight supplies, and we began a regular, flirtatious conversation, each part continuing the next night. We could have gone indefinitely, I suppose, bantering before dawn until one of us got bold. Then one night he mentioned that he was going to be clocking out early, at three instead of five, and he wanted to know if I was free.

"At three?" I asked.

He gave me a smile, as if he understood what an odd sort of time it was for a date. "Working here can make it difficult to keep a regular social schedule," he confessed. "But you seem to like being up at night."

I nodded, feeling him looking me over. I was paint-stained, as always, and a bit dishevelled, but he seemed to like what he saw. "Wanna get a drink?"

"Yeah," I said quickly. "Yeah."

The only thing opened close by besides the grocery store was a convenience store on the corner, so after a brief discussion of our lack of options, we went there for slushees. We sat outside, in the chill pre-dawn air, and I shivered all over as I got that first thrilling headrush of cherry-slushee.

He watched me shudder with the chill, and he grinned and touched my arms. "You don't have to finish it," he said softly.

"I do."

"Why?"

"You bought it for me –"

"And what does that mean?"

"It makes it special."

I don't know why, but he understood that. This was our first date. Three a.m. Outside of a 7-11, following none of the rules that my girlfriends live by. But I have my own set of rules, and I was going to drink that cherry slushee until the ruby-dyed-ice stained my lips dark pink. Until I was shivering all over, cold to the core. Until he put his strong arm around me, holding me tight to his body as I swallowed the last sweet drop. I rested my head on his shoulder, revelling in the warmth of him after devouring such a chilling treat.

"Where to?" he asked softly, speaking against my dark hair.

I knew right then that we were going to fuck. I knew when he bought me the slushee. Jesus, I knew when he said "Wanna get a drink?" Sometimes you know. We were only two blocks away from my place, and I laced my fingers with his, paying attention to how large his hand was. Sure, I know what people say – you can't tell anything from that. But they're wrong. Cock-size and hand-size might not be equateable, but you *can* guess how a large hand might feel against your ass if it were delivering a few stinging strokes of a bare-bottomed spanking. You can gauge from the grip if a man is into control, or more likely to take a backseat roll.

I could tell that he was in charge, even as he let me lead him to my place. I could tell from the way he circled my waist with his arm, from the way that he took my key out of my hands and opened the door for me. He stopped me in the entryway and kissed my sticky cherry lips and said, "I've been thinking about those lips of yours from the first time I saw you."

"Yeah," I teased, "what were you thinking?"

"About how sweet they'd feel around my cock." As he spoke, he pushed me down, his hands firm on my shoulders. I felt my knees bend, felt myself go into that automatic pre-cock sucking position. I was excited, hungry, and curious – watching as he undid the fly of his jeans and let me see him for the first time. I had my face up close, breathing in to smell the faded fabric of his denims, the warmth of his hidden skin. I wanted to suck. I was ready for him, drawing him into the chill of my mouth, still so cold from the slushee, but he didn't care. He warmed me rather than letting me cool him down. He played me, his fingers slipping through my hair, his body pressing back and forth, rocking me, working with me while he spoke.

"God, I couldn't think when I saw you that first time. All covered in paint. So dirty, and you didn't care. You just went out like that."

My girlfriends are the type who polish up before exiting their apartments. Can't be seen without makeup, a blow-dry, an 'outfit.' I've known them all since high school, and we have history together. But we share nothing else.

"I liked that," he said. "I liked that you were mussed, but still so pretty, and you didn't care that there was a blue streak of paint on your cheek, or the fact that your jeans had holes."

He slid in and out of my mouth as he spoke, and I swallowed hard on him, rather than try to keep up my end of the conversation. I would have drained him right there, in the entry to my tiny apartment, if he'd let me. But as I'd gauged from the way his hand gripped mine, he was planning on being in charge. And his idea of the evening – excuse me, the *morning* – didn't end with a blow job by the front door. After letting me wet him with my mouth, he lifted me up, this time in his arms, and carried me down the short hallway to the bedroom.

This was where I painted. A large easel sat in the middle, and my tiny bedroll lay sprawled against one wall. It actually showed how little I cared for the concept of sleep. Now, I wished I had a king-size, something luxurious and dreamy for him to toss me onto. He set me gently, and then looked over my art supplies, his eyes finally setting on a roll of twine I used to tie paper to my finished canvases before transporting them for show.

With a length of twine, he tied me up – wrists together, ankles bound – and then gave me a kiss on the lips. "Be right back," he murmured.

I didn't ask. I just nodded. In five minutes, he'd returned, with another slushee. I trembled all over when I saw it, not sure how I knew what to expect, but expecting just the same. I knew he didn't expect me to drink that, and I knew he wasn't going to sit at my side and slurp up the crushed ice himself. I was right.

While I watched, he drew the slushee in with the straw and used the flavoured ice to decorate my skin – my

175

nipples, my collarbones, a lone line down the basin of my belly.

"Oh, god –" I moaned.

He followed each magic line of the straw with the warmth of his mouth.

"Oh, yes –" I said next.

To my utter delight, he took turns, first drawing designs on my naked skin with the iced cherry confection and then retracing those same patterns with his tongue. I thrashed on the bedroll, made crazy by the combination of the cold and the heat, by the tempting slow way that he worked me. I couldn't decide what it was that I wanted – or more truly, I couldn't fathom that I really wanted what I thought I did. Which was this:

The slushee, that cold, chilling slushee, right on my clit. Oh, yeah, that's what I wanted. Even as I shivered all over, trembling with all my might, I desperately wanted him to lift the straw and streak a line of deep fuchsia iced slushee over my clit.

"Do it," I told him. "Oh, please."

"You really want me to." It wasn't a question. He knew me that well already. It wasn't a question at all. But I answered, despite the lack of querying tone in his voice. I locked my eyes on his, and I licked my bottom lip, and I said. "Yes. Go on. Go on and do it."

I watched him suck a bit of the melting drink up the straw, capture the liquid with his thumb over the tip, and then bring the straw right over my pussy. I thought of how people play with candlewax, straining against the heat, and I wondered which sensation was more pleasurable. I thought of those silly conversations you have when you're a kid, teasing your friends with horror tales: how would you rather die? In fire or in ice? I had time to think those thoughts before he lifted his thumb and released the river of slushed cherry ice over my desperately waiting clit, and then I lifted my hips off the thin make-shift mattress and screamed. The sensation was overpowering. So cold. So fucking cold. Everything in my body tensed, as if my muscles had gotten some message to lock down. Before I could make any noise again, begging, howling, whimpering, crying, he settled himself between my legs and brought his mouth to my pussy and began to lick. Hot against my cold, drinking my juices mixed and mingled with the melted slushee.

As soon as I relaxed into the warmth of his mouth, he reached for the slushee again. I didn't say no. I didn't say yes. I just closed my eyes and held my breath and waited. Again, the coldest river of juices poured over me, and then his mouth followed immediately, warming where the ice had kissed my naked skin. Over and over he dripped and drank until I came, in a cherry-wave of pleasure, bucking and pulling on the twine, knowing I'd have marks on my skin, and not caring one bit. The climax rocked me, and I didn't have the ability to see what was going to happen next, didn't guess that as soon as I came, he'd have another plan.

He did.

He was moving as I came. Instead of using a straw, he scooped iced slushee with his fingers and spread a fingerfull into the mouth of my pussy. I groaned so loud, my eyes open now, watching as he shifted, so that his cock could dive inside of me, where the ice and heat were waiting.

Now, he fucked me. Fucked me with an intensity I couldn't believe. Not only the cherry slushee melted, but I felt as if I melted into him. My body, my fears, my desires. I melted into a pool of sticky syrup, a puddle of slushee from a twenty-four hour market. Who'd ever

177

have guessed that 99 cents could bring a girl that much pleasure?

We ruined the white twin sheets with the staining cherry dye. But I tingle all over when I think back on that night. My girlfriends don't understand when I try to explain these sorts of situations. How I get myself in such sultry messes. What *they'd* consider messes. What I consider sticky-sweet. Because now I don't have any incentive to return to a normal schedule, to sleep from 11 to 7 and go about the day like the rest of the world. I like the midnight hours. I like going to the 24-hour grocery right before he punches out, and then walking hand and hand to the 7-11 for our standard, icy dessert.

None of my friends seem to get the appeal. Maybe I'm crazy. Or maybe I just need a new set of girlfriends. But before that, I need another cherry slushee.

Dangerous Fruitcake
or: **Moist and Delicious,** a Christmas Fable
by Anonymous

"Don't be mean," you tell me. "You know she loves us."

"Of course she does," I say, tearing open the package. "That's why she sends us the same thing every Christmas."

The package comes open and I sit there regarding another fruitcake, a rock solid block of snail-mail granite.

"She bakes it herself!" you say defensively. You're so protective of your aged grandmother – even her fruitcakes.

"Of course she does," I say.

"You've got to taste it fresh," you mutter sadly. "It's delicious."

"I'm sure it's nice when it's fresh."

"It's succulent. Moist and delicious."

I take the fruitcake out of the wrapping, hold it in my hand, pound it against the table.

"Amazing what three weeks in the cargo compartment of a 747 can do to 'moist and delicious.'"

The problem with grandma is that she was raised in the Depression. She mails everything fourth class.

"We have to keep it until Mom comes," you say.

"We'll wrap it in cellophane and put it under the tree. It makes her happy to know we got one, too."

"She likes to share the pain."

"Stop," you say. "She means well."

Hefting the deadly fruitcake, I look at you and smile. It's two Saturdays before Christmas, and you're wearing your weekend lounging-in-bed, drinking-coffee-and-reading-the-New-Yorker clothes. Long white T-shirt, thin with wear, damp with sweat from the hot blow of the space heater. Panties underneath, peeking at me invitingly.

"You wouldn't," you say, clutching your *New Yorker* to your chest.

"I would," I say, and reach for you.

"Let go!" you shout as I seize your shirt, dragging you into the middle of the bed. You start to giggle as I get my arm under yours and perform a neat wrestling move that you'd never let me get away with if you weren't distracted by the fruitcake. I thrust you over my lap and hold you there, pulling up your long white T-shirt and raising the fruitcake like a paddle.

"Moist and delicious, huh? I'll show you moist and delicious!"

The fruitcake comes pounding down, and you yelp as it strikes your buttocks. Rather than the satisfying "slap!" I'm used to, it makes a dull thudding sound. It makes you giggle.

"You're being difficult," you say sharply, fighting through the giggles. "Stop spanking me with my grandmother's fruitcake!"

"You're the difficult one," I say. "Put your ass in the air and take your spanking like a good girl!"

That brings another giggle, and you snuggle deeper into my lap and lift your ass. I bring the fruitcake down, harder this time, and the thud comes firmly enough to make you gasp. Your ass wriggles as you push it higher. You always did prefer thud to sting, and this is the thuddiest implement of all, its hard-baked exterior hitting hard while its thick, gooey insides provide the weight.

I spank you several more times with the fruitcake, and you're not struggling any more. Now my hand is tangled in your hair, holding your face down against the pillow as I hit your ass repeatedly. I can feel my cock growing, pressing against your breasts. You can feel it, too, and you squirm a little, rubbing it. I spank you three more times in rapid succession, bringing soft moans from your lips. The *New Yorker* falls neglected to the carpet in a flurry of glossy paper. Five more spanks, fast and hard, you whimpering and pushing your ass up to greet my blows. The fruitcake leaves oily stains on your white cotton panties.

"Take them off," I tell you.

This time you don't argue, don't struggle, don't even whimper. You squirm in my lap as you pull down your panties to your ankles and kick them across the room.

"The shirt, too," I tell you firmly.

You pull your arms into the stretched-out armholes and wriggle the shirt up to your head, casting it across the pillow. Now you're naked, your bare bottom red and gorgeous in the slanted morning sunlight.

You gasp as I bring the fruitcake down on your naked behind. You push your ass up into the air again, begging for more. You start whimpering as I strike you faster, my cock surging against your breasts. I feel your hand around it, tucked under your body as you slowly stroke me. You moan, your hand tightening on my cock. Your legs slip open wider, your pussy exposed. I turn the fruitcake sideways and strike your pussy with the narrow edge, bringing a shriek and then a long, low moan of pleasure. I hit it more lightly, the edge striking your clit. It's begun to soften with the repeated abuse, and it's just the right texture for your pussy.

You're gasping now, rubbing my cock as you wag your ass back and forth. I hit your pussy rhythmically, knowing just the right timing to bring you close – but not bring you off. You adjust yourself, bending your waist sharply so you can leave your ass high in the air and move your face to my cock. You take it into your mouth, bent at an improbable angle as you start sucking my cock. Each stroke of your tongue brings a harder spank, and I alternate from your pussy to your ass. Both are now shiny with sticky sugar, moist and delicious.

The fruitcake breaks open, falling into a half-dozen pieces on the bed. You barely notice, consumed by your desire for my cock. I push you off me and onto your belly, and your ass rises high into the air as I take my place between your thighs.

I scoop up a pulpy mass of the fruitcake's moist insides and reach around to your face, pushing it into your mouth. You accept it hungrily, chewing and savouring the spicy taste as my cockhead finds your entrance and I push swiftly in, feeling you wet. You're so wet, in fact, that I can feel a dribble leaking onto my balls as I slide all the way into you, and I know you're very close to coming.

Another mass of pulpy flesh finds its way into your mouth, and you lick my fingers as I reach under you with my other hand. To make you come hard in this position, my cock has to work slowly, deliberately, each thrust firm and deep, pressing down and into your G-spot. And my fingers, still sticky and oozing with fruitcake mess, have to press hard on your clit. Your ass works back and forth, pushing you onto me rhythmically, telling me I've found exactly the right spot, exactly the right cadence. You're close. I grab a wad of fruitcake and use the mush to cushion my fingers so I can press harder on your clit, the way I might use a pillow.

You lick the pulp from my fingers, biting down almost hard enough to hurt me as you start to come.

The second I feel your pussy spasming, the instant I know you're over the edge, I start fucking you rapidly, the way you love. You're still coming when I reach my own completion, my muscles tensing as I spurt inside you, mingling my come with your grandmother's fruitcake. Your pumping ass goes slack, easing down until you're laying flat on the bed, fruitcake crushed underneath your hips, me on top of you in an irregular bed of spicy breadstuffs with crispy, dried-out edges.

"No fruitcake under the tree this year," I say sadly.

You turn your head so I can kiss you, and I taste the spice of Grandma's fruitcake.

"Mmmm," I say. "Moist and delicious."

"I got your moist and delicious right here," you say, and reach for me.

About those Juicy Authors

Xavier Acton ("Fuck-Me Fruits") has written for Sweet Life: Erotic Fantasies for Couples, Gothic.Net, and Necromantic.com.

Stephen Albrow ("Table for Two") was born and raised in the sunny seaside town of Lowestoft, England. Walking through its mean streets, he developed an eye, ear and nose for all things sexual and perverse. The things he saw and heard and smelled, he has since used as fodder for a whole host of filthy stories. They can be found in various notorious publications, such as Swank Confidential, Penthouse Variations, Knave and Fiesta Digest.

Ric Amadeus ("Forbidden Fruit") writes erotica for his lovers and friends via the Internet. He goes by various names at various times.

Zoe Bishop ("Spicy Saturday") has written short stories and erotic poetry for such venues as Good Vibes Magazine and Magnifique.

Rachel Kramer Bussel ("Doing the Dishes") lives in New York where she writes about books, sex, smut, and music. She is the reviser of The Lesbian Sex Book, co-author of The Erotic Writer's Market Guide, co-editor of lesbian erotica anthology Up All Night and a nightlife columnist for the New York Blade. She is also a Contributing Editor at Cleansheets.com. Her writing has been published in AVN, Bust, Curve, Diva, Girlfriends, On Our Backs, Playgirl, Rockrgirl, The San Francisco

Chronicle, and in over 20 erotic anthologies including Best Lesbian Erotica 2001, Best Women's Erotica 2003, and Best American Erotica 2004. Find out more at www.rachelkramerbussel.com.

Elizabeth Colvin ("Thanksgiving Dinner") is a journalist with a dirty mind. Colvin has written for Good Vibes Magazine and numerous small zines.

M. Christian ("The Naked Supper") is the author of the critically acclaimed and best selling collections Dirty Words and Speaking Parts. He is the editor of The Burning Pen, Guilty Pleasures, the Best S/M Erotica series, The Mammoth Book of Tales of the Road and The Mammoth Book of Future Cops (with Maxim Jakubowksi), and over 12 other anthologies. His short fiction has appeared in over 150 books including Best American Erotica, Best Gay Erotica, Best Lesbian Erotica, Best Transgendered Erotica, Best Fetish Erotica, Best Bondage Erotica, and ... well, you get the idea. He lives in San Francisco and is only some of what that implies.

Dante Davidson ("Farm Fresh") is the pseudonym of a professor who teaches in Santa Barbara, California. His short stories have appeared in Bondage, Naughty Stories from A to Z, Sweet Life I and II, and Best Bondage Erotica (Cleis). With Alison Tyler, he is the co-author of the best-selling collection of short fiction Bondage on a Budget and Secrets for Great Sex After Fifty (which he wrote at age 28). He dedicates this story to AM.

Shanna Germain ("Amy's Tattoo") is a freelance writer

and editor based out of Portland, Ore. Her creative work has appeared in a variety of publications, including Clean Sheets, Dare, From Porn to Poetry I and II, Good Vibes, and Salon.com.

Benedict Green ("Menthol Attack") is a computer programmer and dabbler in fiction who lives in San Francisco with his girlfriend and their two cats. This is his first published erotic story.

As of writing these self-revelatory lines, **Maxim Jakubowski** ("Dear Alison") is on a Caribbean island, most often in a state of undress, surrounded by beautiful women in a similar state of non-attire. Blame it on sun, sand and food, but this provokes little lust in his heart. However, in civilian life, he lives in London and rides the tides of sex, editing the best-selling Mammoth Book of Erotica anthology series, crime novels full of lust and yearning (latest is 'Kiss me Sadly'), owning a mystery bookshop, organizing film and literary festivals and authoring columns for the Guardian and Amazon.co.uk., whenever his mind is not occupied by matters carnal. His newest novel, *Confessions Of A Romantic Pornographer*, is scheduled to appear this winter.

Matthew Leland ("Sugar Free") is the pseudonym of a marketing executive who recently quit sugar, caffeine, and cigarettes with his girlfriend's help. It didn't really happen exactly like it did in the story, but it was close.

Tyler Morgan ("Eating") has written for anthologies including *Naughty Stories from A to Z, Volume 2* (PTP). Raised in Texas, Mr Morgan now splits his time between

London and Manhattan.

N.T. Morley ("Seven Courses") is the author of more than 20 published and forthcoming erotic novels of dominance and submission, including The Parlor, The Limousine, The Circle, The Appointment, and the trilogies The Office, The Library and The Castle. Morley's recent projects include MASTER and slave, two books of erotic stories available from Venus Book Club.

Isabelle Nathe ("Sweets for the Sweet") has written for anthologies including Come Quickly for Girls on the Go (Rosebud), and A Century of Lesbian Erotica (Masquerade). Her work has appeared on the web site www.goodvibes.com and in the anthology Naughty Stories from A to Z (PTP).

Emilie Paris ("Hunger") is a writer and editor. Her first novel Valentine (Blue Moon) is available on audiotape by Passion Press. She abridged the '7th century novel The Carnal Prayer Mat for Passion Press. The audiotape won a Publisher's Weekly best audio award in the "Sexcapades" category. Her short stories have also appeared in Naughty Stories from A to Z, Volume I (PTP) and in Sweet Life I & II (Cleis) and on the web site www.goodvibes.com.

Jacqueline Pinchot ("All-Day Sucker") has written for publications including Come Quickly for Girls on the Go (Masquerade), Playgirl, and Gone is the Shame (Masquerade).

Julia Price ("Spanish Olive") has written short stories for the anthologies Body Check and Faster Pussycats, both from Alyson Books. She lives in West Hollywood with her lover and their brood of very opinionated cats.

Carol Queen ("Bounty of Summer") has a doctorate in sexology. She works at Good Vibrations in San Francisco and is a much-anthologized and award-winning author and editor of erotica and sexual commentary. She's the author of Exhibitionism for the Shy, The Leather Daddy and the Femme, and Real Live Nude Girl. Visit her bibliography at www.carolqueen.com for more detail.

Jean Roberta ("Melting Chocolate, Crumbling Stone") lives in the extreme climate of the Canadian prairie, where she teaches English at the local university, sings in the local queer choir, and writes. Her partner, family and friends have become resigned to her erotica and opinionated non-fiction. Her lesbian novel, "Prairie Gothic," is in the catalogue of e-publisher Amatory Ink. Her reviews and articles appear regularly on the websites "Slave's Tribute" and "Technodyke".

Thomas S. Roche ("Double Espressos to Go) is the author of more than 200 published short stories that have appeared in many anthologies, magazines, and web sites. His books include the Noirotica series of anthologies, four anthologies of horror fiction, and his own collections Dark Matter and His and Hers (the latter two with Alison Tyler).

Oscar Shemoth ("Hot Tomato") is the evil doppleganger

of a prominent and popular author whose mind finally snapped under the strain of too many appositives, Oscar Shemoth lurks in his remote Yukon lair planning the ruin of the international literary community through a diabolical plan involving leopard-print underwear and mutant heirloom tomatoes from space.

Muahahahaha!

Simon Torrio ("Appetizers") has appeared in the anthologies Sweet Life 2: Erotic Fantasies for Couples and MASTER.

Violet Taylor ("Breakfast in Bed") has written short stories that have appeared in the anthologies Underwater (Roughneck Press) and Faster Pussycats (Alyson Books). She lives in the Los Angeles area with her girlfriend.

Alison Tyler ("Cherry Slushee") is undeniably a naughty girl. With best friend Dante Davidson, she is the co-editor of the best-selling collection of short-stories *Bondage on a Budget*. Her short stories have appeared in anthologies including *Sweet Life 1 & 2*, *Wicked Words 4, 5, 6, & 8*, *Best Women's Erotica 2002 & 2003*, *Guilty Pleasures*, and *Sex Toy Tales*. She is the editor of the series *Naughty Stories from A to Z* (Pretty Things Press) and *Best Bondage Erotica* (Cleis). Her favorite flavour is cherry red.

Sage Vivant ("Juice for Breakfast") is the proprietress of Custom Erotica Source, the home of tailor-made erotic fiction since 1998. She has been a guest on numerous television and radio shows nationwide. Her work has appeared in *Naughty Stories for A to Z* (II and III), *Best*

Bondage Erotica, *Down and Dirty* and featured in *Maxim, Forum UK*, and *Erotica* magazines. She is the co-editor of *Leather, Lace, and Lust* and *Binary* with M. Christian. Visit Custom Erotica Source at www.customeroticasource.com.

Scott Wallace ("Good Fortune") has appeared in Sweet Life 2: Erotic Fantasies for Couples, as well as several small zines and Good Vibes Magazine.

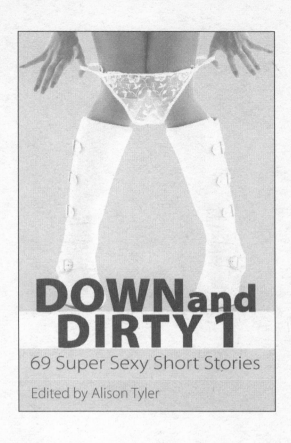

DOWN and DIRTY 1

69 Super Sexy Short Stories

Edited by Alison Tyler

The short stories in this collection are written by some of
the best authors in the business – including M. Christian,
Thomas S. Roche, Sage Vivant, Maxim Jakubowski, Rachel
K. Bussel, N. T. Morley, Dante Davidson, and many more.
Some stories are sensational sexual snippets, while others
are fully detailed dramatic depictions. All of the 69 pieces
have one thing in common: they're dirtier than dirty. And
we know that's just the way you like them!

ISBN 9781906125851 price £7.99

The True Confessions of a London Spank Daddy

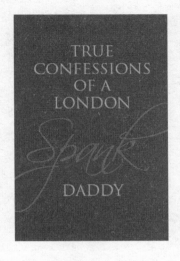

My name is Peter, I'm 55 and I'm a Spank Daddy. I offer a spanking and disciplining service to women...

Discover an underworld of sex, spanking and submission. A world where high-powered executives and cuddly mums go to be spanked, caned and disciplined.

In this powerful and compelling book Peter reveals how his fetish was kindled by corporal punishment while still at school. How he struggled to contain it until, eventually, he discovered he was far from alone in London's vibrant, active sex scene.

What he learnt on the scene helped him to understand the psychology of women who wanted to submit to submissive discipline. Many were professional women, often juggling a demanding job and family. They needed to occasionally relinquish all control, to submit totally to the will of another. Others sought a father figure who could offer them the firm security they remembered from their childhood when Daddy had been very much in control.

Chapter by chapter he reveals his clients' stories as he turns their fantasies into reality. The writing is powerful, the stories graphic and compelling.

Discover an unknown world...

ISBN 9781906373313   Price £9.99

Please visit our website at

www.xcitebooks.com

for free downloads and extracts